DAVID CHRISTOPHER

Tango
Whisky

BB

Bassdrum Books *BB*
Wellington, New Zealand
Bassdrumbooks@mail.com

Copyright: David Christopher © 2018
David Christopher asserts the moral right to be identified as the author
of this work

First Printing: June 2018
ISBN-978-0-473-44004-6

All rights reserved.

No part of this book may be reproduced in any form or by any
electronic or mechanical means including information storage and
retrieval systems, without permission in writing from the author. The
only exception is by a reviewer, who may quote short excerpts in a
review.

This book is a work of fiction. Names, characters, places, and
incidents either are products of the author's imagination or are used
fictitiously. Any resemblance to actual persons, living or dead, events,
or locales is entirely coincidental.

Cover photo courtesy of AppyParking

TANGO WHISKY

Dedicated to Traffic Wardens (or whatever title they have now), the world over. Heroes all!

Chapter One

Reggie Parkes didn't intend to emerge from the West Way underpass in time to see the postman getting shot, but it was increasingly the norm in his life to be the wrong person in the wrong place at the wrong time, so although shocked out of his mind, he wasn't entirely surprised.

"Oh My God!" he muttered as he instinctively attempted to merge back into the gloom of the tunnel. "I've got to get out of this. I'll get shot. That was a gun. It'll be them yardies or whatever." Like most citizens of Westbourne, he had read about yardies only recently in connection with a particularly nasty murder up in London. He didn't really know what a yardie was, but he knew that they used guns and shot people. Drugs or something, and now they had obviously expanded their operations to Westbourne. He ran his finger round the inside rim of his peaked Traffic Warden hat as the sweat dribbled down behind his ears and he loosened his tie which seemed to be squeezing his neck in half.

From the urine smelling damp of the underpass, he could see that the two men, one wielding a gun, frantic in their efforts to get a large satchel off a postman. They had succeeded in getting the strap caught up around the handlebars of the post bike and were pulling, sweating and dragging the whole thing towards what Reggie imagined was the getaway car. The thought of slapping a parking ticket on to the car to somehow delay their escape came briefly into his mind. Tickets were Reggie's weapons of choice and the only car he could see was on a yellow after all. No parking between 10am and 6pm, Monday to Saturday. One hour parking on Sundays. It was midday Tuesday. The car was an old, rusty Hillman Imp. Probably no MOT, he thought. Probably no nothing in fact with bald tyres as well! That total lack of respect for the civilised norms of parking a vehicle really annoyed Reggie.

"The bastards," he mumbled. "No shame at all. Totally out of order, parking that piece of rubbish there on a Tuesday at this hour." His right hand moved instinctively to his ticket book, but as he did so, at that exact moment, his radio burst loudly into life.

"Shitty death," he gasped, trying to reach the volume knob to turn it down. "This bloody radio. Useless when you need it, and now telling the whole bloody world that I'm here."

His frantic mumbling began to take on a high-pitched squeak as he desperately tried to turn the volume down. "Why don't these sodding knobs ever work?" he moaned. "Useless, shitting thing." The radio roared on. A PC warning that Big Edna, Westbourne's favourite lady was gearing up for a lunchtime session at the pub. Edna's lunchtime sessions always carried on into evening sessions, and her evening sessions always, without fail, necessitated strong arm intervention by the police using shock and awe tactics.

At the same moment that the radio told the listening world about the impressive presence of Big Edna, the two gunmen looked up and learned about the somewhat less impressive presence of Reggie.

"Shit," said Reggie still under his breath in the vague notion that if they couldn't hear him they wouldn't see him. But the gun pointing directly at his chest from fifty yards away told him that they did actually know of his presence, and that they didn't welcome it. He turned to go. To disappear back into the tunnel and find somewhere quiet and well out of sight, to radio for help and backup. But too late.

"Well, go on, do something then!" He jumped, as a woman's voice shrieked in his ear. "You're a sort of copper aren't you? You always tell me you are at any rate. So go and arrest them bleeders and stop whining. You sound like one of them muppet things I saw on telly. Beaker. Yeah, that's the one." A small and ugly terrier yapped and growled furiously by her side.

The voice, coming out of nowhere, made his heart miss what seemed like hundreds of beats and his head turned dizzy at the lack of blood. He knew the voice which came from half an inch behind his left ear. 'Silly old bag', he thought savagely as he swung round. 'She must have crept up on me'. Mrs Wellworthy, a moaning old cow from Shelley Mansions, just the other side of the underpass. Never had a ticket. Red Lada Riva. D Reg. Taxed for a year. He even knew the tax disc number. 'Professional, knowing that sort of thing in my business,' he thought.

"Well, go on," she pushed him hard. "Sort them buggers out will you." Her dog Muggins yapped furiously.

"You stupid cow," oathed Reggie as he stumbled out of the underpass into the full glare of the sun and the hostile stare of the two gunmen. For a brief, blissful millisecond, his mind produced a picture of him slapping a ticket and a no tax disc warning on Mrs Wellworthy's Lada, but the hard barrel of the small revolver suddenly jabbing into his neck brought him back to the horrible reality of his immediate situation. He hadn't even noticed the robber approaching him. The robber was fat and shaven headed, and to Reggie had the sort of ugliness that could only mean that the man was a murderous bastard who should have been locked up at the age of ten with all his mates, and the key thrown away. Mrs Elworthy had miraculously moved out of sight into the dark recess of the underpass.

"It's a soddin Traffic Warden," shouted ugly features. "Not a copper arter all. What we gonna do wiv im then Lenny? 'Ere, you. Traffic Warden shithead. Get yer arse over there. Where the postie is. Go on or I'll give yer an effing boot up the jacksie." Reggie stared at the man in horror, unable to move, and so true to his word, Ugly gave Reggie a hard kick in the rear end to help him on his way, and Reggie, half scrabbling and half running launched himself over to the postman, any attempt at maintaining dignity under the gaze of Mrs Wellworthy now completely out of the window. 'Sod Mrs Wellworthy', he thought.

"Are you all right mate," grunted the postman, as Reggie flopped down next to him.

"No I'm bloody well...." Reggie stopped suddenly as the realisation hit him that here was a man with gun wounds asking him if he was OK. Compared to that poor sod, of course he was OK.

"And yes, I'm OK as well," muttered the postman reading Reggie's thoughts. "Nearly got a bullet in my leg though. Look, just here." He pointed out through the tear in his trousers the small but deeply oozing wound caused by the bullet passing by. "The silly sod nearly missed total like, but just got me. It's just a scratch really, but it hurts like hell and I feel really faint. Did you press your panic call button?" his voice dropped to a whisper.

Reggie's head nearly hit the ground. "The panic call button," he moaned. "The panic call. What with Mrs Wellworthy shouting at me and one thing and another, I...."

"Come on you bastard," yelled ugly, breaking into Reggie's whining excuses, "givus yer radio. Don't want yer tellin tales now to the world do we? Come on Lenny, let's grab the radio and piss off quick. We've got the bag." He leaned down and grabbed at the radio on Reggie's belt and tugged hard, his small black pistol inches from Reggie's head. At this stage, Reggie would have willingly given him the thing if it meant him and his mate buggering off. Indeed, he tried to help him free the radio from the awkward belt clip, twisting the belt round to get a better grip.

"What yer doing?" growled Ugly pulling the thing back again. "Don't bugger about or I'll cosh yer one." He pulled harder on the radio, growing angrier and angrier at its refusal to come off the belt, and finally gave a huge yank on the thing in his frantic attempt to remove it. This violent movement momentarily brought Reggie's forehead smashing into his nose with the rest of Reggie thrashing around like an eel on a hook. With a shriek, Ugly rushed his hands to his bloodied nose, dropping Reggie like a sack to the ground, and dropping his pistol down next to him.

"Grab the gun," shouted the postman. "Pick the bloody thing up. Quick!"

Through the haze and confusion of his by now hugely overstretched mental faculties, Reggie saw the pistol lying there and leapt at it, just as the police car siren shrieked in the next street.

"They're getting away," shouted the postman, as Ugly's mate fled the scene. "They've got my bag. Go on shoot the bastards. Go on man shoot them for fu….."

The pistol went off as Reggie rolled over intending to take aim as he had seen the cops do on TV. Grabbing the Postman's bag from which a small brown envelope fell to the ground, Ugly raced off up the road after his mate just as Reggie's bullet blew the street lamp above them into pieces, of which the largest landed fairly and squarely on Reggie's head, as he rose from the ground.

"Shit," moaned Reggie before collapsing back into the gutter.

"Prat," muttered Mrs Wellworthy as she bent over to retrieve a small packet that she saw on the ground lying next to Reggie. "If I hadn't called the police, I hate to think what would've happened. I suppose I'd better look after this envelope for the silly sod though. It might be important."

Had she known the consequences of that small act of kindness, Mrs Wellworthy might well have kicked the packet into the nearby drain and never mentioned the subject again.

Chapter Two

Reggie knew he was a hero even before the first visit from the head Traffic Warden. The nurse had told him so.

"Well Mr Parkes," she said briskly, "you are a bit of a hero you know. Saving the postman's life and foiling those awful robbers. It's all over the papers you know. Every detail." She peered closely at Reggie's face. "Hold still now while I get these bits of glass out." Reggie winced as she expertly plucked another piece of street lamp from his face.

"You'll have a bad scar here I'm afraid Mr Parkes. Right down your cheek. Just like them swordsmen in the old films. You know, Zoro and the three muskets and epics like that. Dead romantic! And you're under police protection too. At least until they've questioned you about the robbery."

"Oh dear," sighed Reggie, secretly thrilled to bits by the thought of it all. In the news. Police protection. A vivid scar. After a heroic action. Guns. A permanent reminder to all those other bloody piss taking bastards in the Traffic Warden crew room of his heroism and bravery. A wound even. And not an ordinary wound either. Not the sort of wound you could get in a small accident like falling off a bike or cutting yourself in the tool shed, or even being hit by someone. This was a wound received on active service; Traffic Warden Service. A proper, fighting wound! If fanatical terrorists had been involved it would have been a tiny bit more hero like, but crazed gunmen would do just fine.

After the nurse had finished her ministrations, and bound his face, he lay back on his pillow and thought over the events of the day, his rather embarrassing and very rare hard on dying with the departure of the nurse. To be honest, he couldn't really remember everything about it. He'd been too shit scared and..... ..."Oh bollocks," he groaned. Talking of shit. "Ah, nurse," he called as she was about to leave the room. "Er..my trousers, and er...under things...you know..."

"Don't worry yourself about them, Mr Parkes," she cut in smiling. "That happens to many people when they get bashed unconscious. Purely a biological reaction. It happens to all heroes you know. It's the bit that never gets in the papers. Your clothes have been clean and ironed and are over there in the wardrobe. No need to mention it again. Bye for now." She strode off briskly. Her ministrations needed by many others that day.

'Thank God for that,' he thought as he lay back down into his pillow, knowing that his little accident had actually happened long before the bloody great bit of street lamp landed on his head. That nurse though, he thought. Right little cracker. Legs and everything! He lay back; a smile on his face. He wished his niece Roxy was here to see him, but apparently she was on some big job up in London. She'd be really proud of him. He could never understand how his dear departed sister and her fly-by night husband had produced a creature of such beauty and pureness of thought and deed. The Parkes family were definitely not known for their looks, but Roxy was a stunner, and for some reason, adored her uncle Reggie. He could never figure that out either. He really wished she was here to see him now. A hero. Never mind, he thought sleepily. Plenty of time to see her next time she's down this way. She'd be pleased for him.

The police constable at the door, glanced in to check on his temporary charge and looked at the rather scruffy 40ish something man lying there with a smile on his face. He turned back quickly to feast his eyes on the far more appealing sight of dozens of young nurses going about their business.

Reggie dozed and woke; dozed and woke, and each time he woke, he was secretly pleased with himself. A hero. With a wound to prove it. A visible wound! He just hoped though that his old mum had remembered to feed and water his two chinchillas, Star and Mercury. Good names those he thought. They meant something. Universal. They were fine little animals, but needed a lot of attention. He was devoted to the little beasts and had once read that they were crepuscular rodents, slightly larger and more robust than ground squirrels, and he was fascinated to learn that they were native to the Andes Mountains in South America, and that they lived in colonies called "herds." Bit like cows really he thought, only smaller and a bit more rat like. But the very thought of these peaceful little cow like creatures in their little house on the bench in the small out house in his garden was making him sleepy, and with pleasant thoughts of his old mum, his niece Roxy, Star and Mercury, and his wound, he fell deeply asleep.

Barbara Ancaster was the first 'colleague' to look in on hero Reggie. Her position as head Traffic Warden gave her an insight into many of Reggie's little and large peccadilloes, and she knew beyond a doubt that he was no hero. But the evidence was there she thought as she marched purposefully through the hospital. Reggie had confronted armed robbers, wrested a gun off one of them and by all accounts had scared them off by trying to shoot at them. Well so the Westbourne Gazette said anyway. It was bad enough with all the extra security because of the party conference at the Winter Gardens. She was having to deploy wardens into what were usually police patrol areas and now here was Reggie messing about with wounds, and getting the whole team worked up about gunmen on the streets.

Her first view of him confirmed her initial thoughts. It was unmistakably Reggie. Fast asleep, slack jawed, tongue sticking out and dribbling. But he undoubtedly had a wound if all that bandaging meant anything, and a brief flash of irritation furrowed her brow.

"Are you proud of your hero then?" asked the same young duty nurse coming out of her small office at the start of the ward. "I must say he doesn't look all that impressive now" she added doubtfully. "But a credit to the Traffic Wardens all the same."

She looked at Barbara as if for confirmation, but was met only by a blank and vaguely hostile stare. She withdrew hurriedly into her office. She never did like Traffic Wardens really, and this imposing cow seemed to sum up all the horrors in her mind about them.

"This is a bloody nightmare," mumbled Barbara, half to herself and half to the world at large. He's a bloody nightmare already, and now he's going to be a total bloody nightmare. I really can't believe he did all this."

Reggie remained asleep, the vivid wound almost glowing through the bandage as a beacon to his heroism. Barbara turned about to return to the office. She had done her duty by coming to see him. Thankfully, he was asleep. It would have to be another day. If only he hadn't got that wound she thought bitterly. Its existence would be brought into play on every conceivable occasion. It would be included in every conversation. It would be used as evidence of Reggie's superior knowledge about everything each time there was an argument, discussion or dispute about anything in the crew room. She could hear him now. "You're all bloody wrong," he would say. "I know about these things. What do you think I've got on my face? Scotch mist? I didn't get this wound not knowing about things you know. Yeah, well don't you bloody tell me about Traffic Warden duties. I've got a wound mate………………"

And so it would go on; and on; and on! She could see it all, as plain as the bandage on Reggie's face. This whole business was going to be a complete and utter pain in the arse and she had her own problems in that direction without Reggie adding to them.

"Ah well" she mumbled out loud, "a fatal infection might yet set in." Smiling broadly at the thought, she strode purposely back to the Police HQ and the security and calm of her office.

Much to his surprise, Reggie's second visitor was Mrs Elworthy herself. He had woken up by this time and as she came in, he looked at her suspiciously from under his blanket and wondered what the hell she was visiting him for.

"Hero my arse!" were her first words. "Reggie Parkes. You prat around shitting yourself witless and messing about with armed robbers and you end up a hero. Well, if anyone asks me, I'll tell 'em a thing or two, don't you worry. You dropped this, by the way, when you was floundering around on the ground. The ink's run as it's got wet and I can't read the name and address, but I s'pose it must be yours."

She handed him a small, thin, very damp brown packet, more an envelope than anything else, muttered that she supposed she had better wish him well, and flounced out. At least she didn't bring that little horror Muggins with her, he thought.

Reggie, who had said nothing during the entire barrage of words, gingerly got out of bed, shuffled across to his wardrobe and stuffed the envelope into his extremely clean and neatly pressed trouser back pocket. He was too tired and dozy to even think about it now, and he had a hell of a headache. He couldn't remember any envelope at the time, but he supposed the bump on the head had made him forget about things. Anyway, he thought, 'I'll sort it all out tomorrow.' As he was up, he went to the patient's phone at the nurse's office and rang home to make sure his mum was OK, and that Star and Mercury were being fed properly. It would be no good if they suffered, and his mum was at best erratic in remembering to do anything, let alone go to the garden shed and feed the chinchillas.

The Westbourne Gazette, evening edition, in an article written by the new cub reporter Jennifer Johnson, reported that Mugsy Brennan and Lenny Bigglesworth, the perpetrators of the violence against Reggie and the postman, were not the brightest of crooks, nor the most loyal. Unable to start their Hillman Imp get-away car, they had been forced to run, and their almost immediate arrest was occasioned by their entering the Wagon and Horses on their way back to Mugsy's mum's place, sweating and heaving and still carrying what was obviously a heavy post bag. Standing at the bar, they had not finished their first pint when four policemen, summoned by the landlord, entered the pub, nabbed them there and then and retrieved the still full bag. At the preliminary magistrates hearing the next day, it transpired that they had stolen the bag on behalf of a certain Ken Jones, well known villain and local fence who had received intelligence that the bag contained a transit package of diamonds. His intelligence was correct. The diamonds were still in their small and innocuous package in the bag and were safely retrieved by the police. Mugsy's complaint that his gun had been stolen by the Traffic Warden was dismissed and both he and Lennie received eighteen months in the jug. Ken Jones claimed he hadn't seen either of them in his life and hadn't a clue what they were talking about. In the absence of any firm evidence to the contrary, he was released without charge.

It was another two weeks before Reggie was allowed back to the office. In a vain attempt to delay the inevitable, Barbara had offered him an extended period of sick leave, but Reggie, the newly wounded hero, would have none of it. "Sick leave, " he expostulated angrily. "Sick leave? What the hell do I want sick leave for. Can't give out tickets on sick leave. I want to get back to work." Silly cow he thought. I'll show them a thing or two about sick leave! I've got a wound.

Two weeks later, after delaying slightly so as to ensure that there would be plenty of Traffic Wardens present in the office; Reggie strode proudly into the crew room and straight into a blazing row concerning the soft bananas in the female toilet.

Chapter Three

Jan had got up late again as usual. Her well-practised octopus act around the bathroom, grabbing clothes, toothpaste, tampax and everything else she needed as she went was suddenly interrupted by the phone. "Sod it," she oathed. "Who the hell can that be at 6.30 in the morning? Must be important. Probably about the conference."

Barbara had given her the job of operational controller for Traffic Warden deployments during the party conference and she knew it would all be a pain in the arse, evidently starting now. She shoved the phone at her ear.

"Jan. Listen. Did you go into the toilet after me yesterday? You know, down in the office."

"Henrietta, is that you? What the hell do you want at this hour of the morning? I'm trying to clean my teeth for heaven's sake."

"That bit of stuff in the loo. You know! The brown bit on the floor. Well....."

"I thought that was a bit of shit or something" Jan interrupted through the toothpaste. "That's what you get in toilets. It'll get cleaned up. Anyway, is this about deployments or the conference?"

"What? No. I mean the stuff on the floor near the door! Of course it wasn't what you said. Just a bit of banana that had gone brown. They go like that you know, then turn soft and go brown, and look like...well you know,...what you said."

"Yeah, shit. I got some on my shoe," interrupted Jan again applying neutral tint coverall to the bright boily thing on her cheek.

"Well anyway, call it what you want," went on Henrietta, rattled by Jan's less than interested replies. "It wasn't that. It really was banana. But it wasn't one of mine you know. I don't like soft bananas. My Bill always tells me to buy hard, firm ones, at least eight inches long. I only like hard, firm ones....

'I bet you do' wondered Jan, trying desperately hard not to visualise Henrietta with a hard, firm eight inch banana, but feeling just a tiny bit randy about the whole idea of a firm, eight inch banana. "Bugger, it's bleeding now."

"What! Are you listening or not Jan? This is important. It really wasn't mine. I simply can't put soft ones in my mouth. They go all flowery and oozy you know. My Bill doesn't like them all soft either. Anyway, my Bill said I'd better speak to someone about this because......."

"Henrietta!" exploded Jan. "I'm late. I've got deployments to sort out. I've burst a zit. I haven't taken the dog for a walk, and I've got to go to the loo. Now what do you want, because at this moment I don't give a shit about your Bill's hard bananas, or the stuff on the bog floor, and I really don't care what you can or can't put in your mouth. Now what the hell do you want?"

"You really can be vulgar Jan," giggled Henrietta, I've told you. It's about the bit of soft brown banana on the loo floor. Well, I heard Polly tells Barbara that it was me that did it. Well, I ask you, how could it have been me? Me and my Bill don't have soft ones like that. My Bill always says to me that I really must buy...."

"I know" shrieked Jan in total exasperation, cutting straight across, before Henrietta went through the whole thing again. "Hard, firm ones. Henrietta, I'm putting the phone down. I'll talk to you about it in the office. Good bye."

"But Jan......Well! We must have been cut off. These wretched phones. Oh well, I'll have a quiet word later on in the office. Probably better that way. Before the briefing."

Having put the phone down and completed the rest of her ablutions, Jan drove like a maniac to get to work on time, but she drove like a careful maniac. As the first woman driver of an F3 car five years earlier, she was in a class of her own where driving was concerned and it was only a very foolish - and temporary, romantic attachment, and a subsequent move to the Spanish Costas, that had prevented her from moving up the ladder to be the first female F1 driver in the world. But even her skills at the wheel and the souped up engine in her venerable and much admired MGB GT were no match for a lorry load of iron pipes shed all over the dual carriageway. She sat and fumed and waited, knowing that Barbara would be furious at her late arrival at the morning briefing.

The Traffic Warden parade room where the morning briefing took place was a small affair, and in order to get her seat nearest to the head Traffic Warden, Polly usually arrived as early as possible. In order to irritate Polly, Henrietta had arrived even earlier and taken the seat first. No one was going to accuse her of messing up the loo floor with anything. How dare she? Henrietta launched her attack immediately Polly entered the room.

"Now look here Polly, what the hell do you mean by telling everyone that I made a mess in the loo. It was plain malice. Everyone knows it couldn't have been me. My Bill always tells me to use hard ones you know, so how on earth....."

"What the hell are you on about Henrietta? You made that mess and you cleared it up - or most of it, so what's the problem. I don't want you accusing me of...."

"Accusing You. I'm not accusing anyone, you pompous cow Polly."

"Right!" cut in Polly leaping up from her chair. "That's it..."

Reggie's grand arrival at this point was entirely ignored and despite pushing his face forward, vivid scar with stitches well to the fore, he had to shout to get the attention he felt he deserved as a hero.

"What the hell is going on in here?" he bellowed. "I could hear you both half way up the street. Don't talk to me about bananas. I know all about bananas. What do you think this is......"

"Oh sod off Reggie," shouted Polly. "This is none of your bloody business so butt out." She resumed her counter attack on Henrietta, still firmly anchored to the favoured chair.

"What on earth is going on?" Barbara rarely had to raise her voice to anyone, let alone to other Traffic Wardens, but she didn't get to be head warden by being a wimp. Now her voice cut through the loaded atmosphere like a crudely aimed club hammer. "Polly, Henrietta. Sit down, both of you. A bit of decorum, please. I said, Sit Down. Both of you. Now."

"But....."

"I don't care Polly, now sit down and shut up." Polly glared over at Henrietta, whose huge smirk was almost too much for her. She subsided into her seat whilst the onlookers, cheated of their sport, settled down to await their morning brief.

She looked round the room wearily and noticed Reggie sitting in his usual place near the back. 'Oh God,' she thought. 'It's one sodding thing after another today', and she began her briefing.

"Now first of all we must welcome Reggie back to the fold," began Barbara, glancing around furiously at her assembled troops. It was bad enough having Reggie back, without Polly and Henrietta causing mayhem as well. "And of course we all congratulate you on your actions Reggie which were a credit to the Traffic Warden team." Get that bit out of the way first she thought and try and get everything back to normal.

"I don't want no thanks Barbara," began Reggie determined to milk his return back to work for all its worth. "But I must say, it hasn't been easy. I'll have mental scars for the rest of my life. When you are faced with a gun being waived in your face by hardened criminals, I tell you, it was hard even for me to keep calm, but, well, you know one has to do ones best in........."

"Yes, well, we'd better get on Reggie. You're a true hero, we all know that. It said it in the papers."

"Ah, but you don't know everything what happened. Them papers don't know the half of it. Why, when I saw that gun and the poor postie fighting for his life, I thought, right Reggie......."

"Reggie," butted in an increasingly irritated Barbara. "Let's just get the briefing done shall we, then you can inform those of us on office duty, the true facts of it all." She groaned inwardly, but rushed on desperately trying to keep the subject off Reggie.

"As you all know, the Party conference starts tomorrow in the Winter Gardens and so security is quite tight in the town, and we are very much involved in that. The Prime Minister himself will open the show and so obviously the police are very much tied up with it all, and we'll be asked to stand in for many of their routine tasks, so remember that all of you. Jan, wherever she is," she looked round and saw no Jan, "will be in charge of deployments on those conference days if she can bother to turn to work that is. Now Pete, if you could cover area 8, remember that the cones are out along most of Eldridge Road because of the drain men working there, and 'er Dennis, if you could cover area 6 and keep an eye on Park Avenue South. We've had a series of complaints there about car selling from the street, and, oh yes,........."

"Street selling, eh" cut in Reggie. "Now those lads need a talking to and I'm just the man......"

"Reggie, I'll finish the morning brief first if you please. Now where was I. Oh yes, Dave and Dan, you're on van duty so that means cones of course. Take a look at the updated cone map in the office so you'll know where to start placing them, and I suggest you start in Exeter Street as the builders want to get started on demolishing Exeter House as soon as possible."

"Those bloody builders," began Reggie, "I'll 'ave you know that………" His new tirade was mercifully ended by the sudden and noisy arrival of Jan.

This would normally have been a reason for at least a glare of disapproval from Barbara but today it was a welcome distraction from trying to keep Reggie quiet and without giving her a second glance, she carried on with her briefing, but then looked round in annoyance at yet another interruption.

"Urgent call for you Barbara. In the office. I'll put it through."

Barbara looked up from her order sheet in annoyance at Doris the mouse, the small, mousy but persistent little receptionist who manned the outer desk with the immigration people, but brightened as she turned towards the office. 'At least that's over with,' she thought and shouted over the hubbub in the crew room for everyone to get on with it. "Dan, take over the roster. I'd better answer this."

She sat down wearily in her chair; her own personal chair purchased many years ago to ease the persistent eruptions of piles and herpes that plagued her, usually on Monday mornings after a weekend at home on the red wine. She picked up the phone and her brief moment of cheerfulness disappeared as she heard the well-known, doleful tones of Detective Inspector Barney Brightwell; smarmy, arrogant; pig headed and easily the equal of Reggie the hero if it ever came to a complete pain in the arse competition. He was usually known as Dibbs or Dibsey, Officer Dibble or even Officer Dribble to the rest of the world.

"Inspector," she said wearily while trying to sound cheerful and unconcerned about life. "How can I help you?"

"It's 'Detective' Inspector, Barbara as you well know," he launched acidly. He liked Barbara as much as she liked him, which wasn't at all, and he didn't want any crap this morning from a bloody Traffic Warden. "I need to speak to one of your wardens."

Barbara heard the sound of papers rustling and then falling to the floor.

"Which one? I've got quite a lot of them"

"Ah yes, it's your resident hero, Reggie Parkes. I need to speak to him today. Is he in?"

"He's in, so what's it about?"

"Can't say much at the moment. All a bit hush-hush, but apparently there's more to this postman robbery than meets the eye and Reggie seems to be in the middle of it all. London has got involved and until further notice, we are loosely re-classifying him as an accessory to terrorism as it were rather than local hero. I'm afraid he'll have to come down to the Parksdown West station as that's where we are at the moment while our corridor is being painted. So if you could get hold of him that would be good. A policeman from London wants to talk to him at 10.30 on the dot. Evidently something else apart from the diamonds from that post bag didn't arrive where it should have done and they are keen to know if your man knows anything about it. Apparently they think he does and it's to do with a security matter. I'll be present to see fair play, don't worry. Oh! And keep your mouth shut on this one. We do not want any of this to get out to the press. We need to keep a lid on it. OK? Anyway, I've just been called out so got to go." He put his phone down with a bang.

Less than a minute later the phone rang again. A new voice. "Is that Barbara Ancaster?"

"Speaking."

"Ah, Barbara, my name is Percy Smythe. Working with the Met Police and all that. DI Brightwell might have spoken about me. I'm most afraid there's been a small change of plan. We need to get back to London fairly soon-ish - more problems than you can shake a stick at in our line." He chuckled unctuously down the phone which immediately made Barbara hate him. "Anyway, we would be most grateful if Reggie could come down right away for a small chat. The car should arrive outside your place about now with my driver Stan in it, and we can get this over with by hopefully 10. Can you spare him now? Good. Most grateful madam. I'm sure we can settle this soon. Wouldn't want to have to take Reggie away would we now?" Barbara flinched. In that last sentence, his voice had suddenly taken on a hard edge, although the thought of them taking Reggie away wasn't an unpleasant one.

"Oh, and Barbara, I do expect your very full and immediate cooperation. OK?" He put the phone down.

For a long moment, Barbara stayed frozen in her seat, still holding the phone in her right hand. She slowly turned it towards her and mouth open, she stared at the earpiece as if expecting hobgoblins to come out of it and ravage her. Her left hand opened the desk drawer and fumbled around for her tube of pile cream that she now urgently needed before another moment passed. She slowly and painfully rose, carefully replaced the phone on its cradle and walked to the ladies. She noticed a small lump of what looked like shit on the floor of the toilet as she entered the cubicle and on any other day, this sight would have triggered a major and very cross tempered investigation, but just at that moment it merely entered into a catalogue of other outrages that had been sent to plague her week, and anyway, she had far more urgent ministrations to perform if she was to get through the rest of the day without falling to pieces. She brightened a bit and sent for Reggie. At least it would get him off her hands for half the morning.

Little did she know that it would be a lot longer than that and that it would embroil her troops in a chaos not seen in the Westbourne Traffic Warden Service since!

Chapter Four

"Excuse me." I say there, excuse me." Dave Keenan turned around wearily. He knew exactly what was coming. A cone complaint. "Yes, madam. How can I help you?"

Dave, along with all other Traffic Wardens was very polite. 'It's not what you think, it's what you say that counts in dealing with the public'. He heard the words of the head Traffic Warden zap through his neurons as a warning as he turned to face the woman. She was in an elegant green outfit with matching hat and shoes, and he could certainly see that in her younger days, she would have been quite something to look at. She wasn't bad even now!

"It's this ticket," she said almost conversationally, giving one of those dazzling all American type smiles that showed her perfectly aligned teeth off to perfection. "Why have you given it to me? I haven't parked illegally."

"You have actually madam," replied Dave wearily. "Those cones mean no parking. Are you the red Volvo?" he added.

"Yes, but those cones weren't there when we parked. We've just come out of church."

"They were madam. They've been there all night. We put them out at 6 O'clock yesterday evening because of the parking restrictions in place for the party conference. There is a high security alert put out by the police, and we are responding."

As he said it, he knew it wouldn't make any difference. When it came to cones, the great British public were cone blind. They didn't see them; they didn't take any notice of them when they did and even if you stuffed one up their backside and said "This is a bloody police no parking cone. It means don't bloody well park here," they would still get confused about the issues involved and end up with a ticket. Firmness and total obduracy was the answer and Dave got into firm and obdurate mode.

"Madam. We put the cones out last night. They were here when we passed earlier this morning. They are still here now. Your car is parked amongst them and has been so for at least twenty minutes. You have committed an offence. I have given you a ticket telling you this. It is a fixed penalty offence and will cost you £20. If you feel hard done by please write to the ticket office and complain. My number is on the ticket. Good day madam."

He had trotted this speech out on many occasions in the past, and he knew this wouldn't be the end of the matter. It never was with cones.

"Excuse me please. What's all this about?" A pleasant voice. Her husband. "You know old fellow, you really shouldn't persecute white middle class church goers. You police people are going to need our support one day. Now rip the ticket up, there's a good chap."

Poor blacks would be OK, I suppose thought Dave, or Asians. I wonder what he'd think about giving a ticket to a Jap. Perhaps yellow is OK. "I'm sorry, sir." Replied Dave. "I've issued the ticket for good reasons and can't withdraw it. I've explained to your wife that she can complain if she wants to. Good day, sir."

"I don't think you quite understand me young man. Those cones weren't here earlier and you are going to withdraw the ticket. It's no good persecuting us you know." The voice was menacing. His wife tried to pull him to the car. But he returned to the attack.

"Now listen sir. If you continue in this way you'll have to speak to a constable who may not be so impressed with your attitude. There is heightened security in the town at the moment because of the party conference. As you know, there have been terrorist threats against the government and we can't take any chances. Do you want to speak to a constable?"

"Don't start threatening me with constables Mr Traffic Warden. I want to speak to the Chief Constable. Give me his telephone number and address."

"Well, I can't get the Chief Constable at the moment, only an ordinary one, and anyway it's a she. The Chief Constable I mean."

The man visibly paled and looked aghast at his wife.

"Did you hear that? A she! The bloody Chief Constable is a woman Chief Constable? No wonder it's all gone to pot down here. Come Daphne let's get back to London. Fast. I'll be writing to her don't you worry."

This last was hurled at Dave from the car window as the latest edition red Volvo estate sped off to where the Chief Constable was white and male and all was well with the world. If only she'd been a black Chief, thought Dave idly his imagination starting to run with the game. An immigrant black lesbian from a council estate who used to be a bloke. That would have done it. And talking of lesbians he thought as he turned to walk back to the cone wagon and watched with amusement as he saw Jenny Pride striding past with a Rottweiler in the shape of a Gray haired little old lady attached to her ankles.

"I'm never going to help the police again. How dare you persecute old age pensioners? I've been to church you know. I'm going to write and complain about you. I'm not scared of terrorists. We fought in the war you know....."

"Are you OK Jenny," called Dave as the duo sped past.

"Yeah, fine thanks Dave," grinned Jenny looking down at her tormentor. "A cone casualty. I'll shake her off soon. By the way, Dave, there's been a lot of radio traffic this morning hasn't there? Sounds as if there's a bit a flap on, or developing at any rate. Something about Reggie. D'you know anything?"

"I've heard nothing" replied Dave, feeling his belt for his radio. He reddened slightly as he realised he'd left it in the van. That was the trouble with working from the van with cones. Radios simply got in the way when jumping in and out of the vehicle to put down cones. Both Dan and Dave just tended to leave them in the van."

"That's the trouble with you people you know," interrupted the little old lady, looking up at Dave. "Always on the radio, you lot are and not looking after us old folk who fought in the war. Shame on the lot of you!"

With that, she detached herself from Jenny and beetled off back up the road towards her ticketed car. "Wow, that's a relief. Thanks Dave. Anyway, I'd better get on. I've got to get down to the square next."

Dave waved as Jenny wondered off. Shame she's a lezzy, he thought idly. She got a cheeky little face. Quite nice really. With that thought in his head, he turned to cross the road and made his way back to the van. Despite the hassle, cone duty was a peaceful way of passing the day, well away from the chaos of the office from where he was hearing the usual shit and aggro over his radio. Something about Reggie, he heard. Needing to report in as soon as possible. He didn't know Reggie well, but always regarded him as decent sort as long as you could stop him talking, which wasn't often and because of this, he usually avoided him. Now of course, the man was a hero and even if Dave didn't think of him in this mould, he at least acknowledged bravery when he saw it. 'Ah well' he thought, whatever Reggie is up to, won't affect us, and that's something.'

Back in the van, Dan Foster was waiting and thinking. Cones, were not Dan's favourite items either. And he was a fairly senior Traffic Warden. He knew what he had to do with them and he knew what he'd like to do with them. The two were not always the same. But on Traffic Warden mobile, cones were a feature of life. Despite his hatred of the things, he regarded each of the fifty or so cones in the back of his van as his own. They were Police cones and they meant something. They weren't the red jobs that blew all over motorways and got in everyone's way. They were yellow and meant a ticket if anyone messed with them. Anyone wanting to borrow them, had to have a bloody good reason and to these special people, Dan doled them out carefully. In groups of one.

Now with the party conference about to start, he knew he had to keep some in reserve, just in case of sudden emergency. To head terrorists off and stuff like that, he thought idly. He wasn't too sure in his mind exactly what he would exactly do with the cones to keep terrorists at bay, but just having them in reserve was a comfort.

To Dave Keenan, Dan's usual partner in the van, this obsession with cone power was something he didn't exactly share. He'd been accused of persecution with cones; he'd seen cones hurled at him; cones used as hats; cones crushed by angry motorists and on one early Saturday morning he'd even seen cones decorating a tall fir tree in the winter gardens with an artistry that displayed a cultural yobbery of the first order. Despite his less than reverent attitude to cones, Dave knew well from experience that they aroused high passion in the vast majority of the public and needed to be taken seriously. He also knew that Dan's father had been a policeman, and Dan had inherited his utmost respect for the police and for law and order. The police could do no wrong, and if they did, there was a good reason for it, even if they couldn't tell anyone about it. He did temper it with common sense though so he wasn't entirely blind to the small faults of that great organisation.

Dan was glaring at him. "You've took your time Dave, we've no time for arguing with the public. Let's get on with it. We'll 'ave to put them cones down in Argyll Road first," he muttered in his special cone reverent voice. "Them buggers there've apologised for hurling the damned things at Keith yesterday. Mind you, they fetched 'im a right cracker up the arse with one of 'em. You should 'ave seen it. Keith went off in a right 'uff. Daft bugger. He deserved it though. Mind you" he prodded Dave for emphasis, "they shouldn't 'ave used police cones. Especially not them new ones. No bloody respect, them buggers."

The workmen that Dan was referring to were already on site in Argyll Street as the cone van arrived. Without the cones they couldn't stop every Tom, Dick and Harry parking along the street where the building material delivery lorries parked up. Trouble came when the lorries finished their business and went. The building workers then used the coned off space to park their own cars, which were then parked illegally, and received tickets. Two days earlier, Keith, seeing just such a situation totally screwed up by attempting to give the workmen a sound bollocking.

"I've told you bloody lot before about this," he thundered. The cones are for the lorries, not your cars. Now move the bloody things. Now."

"Yer what?" Answered the largest of the group of large, shaven headed brickies and scaffolders. "What yer gonna do about it then. Hah?"

"You lot want tickets. I'll give you tickets," replied the now too committed Keith, and advanced on the cars. "These are police cones and you lot know bloody well that you can't park in cones. That's why you've got the sodding things."

"So if the cones weren't here, anyone could park here," shouted the lead builder.

Not seeing the trap, Keith answered with devastating logic. "But they are here, aren't they."

"Not if we shove 'em up yer arse yer prat." thundered the builder. "ere 'ave one." As he and his mates by now fully armed and equipped with cones, advanced on Keith, realisation hit him that his book of tickets was unlikely to be of much use, given the indelicate nature of the situation, and the rough nature of the brickies in question. He turned and ran. Just as the first cone hit him where intended. The rest flew short as he increased his speed to the corner of the street.

"A sad business that," muttered Dave. "In that only one hit the target that is. I'd have loved to have seen Keith shooting off round the corner with a cone up his arse. But I'll give him his due. He's plucky, taking that lot on, on his own. Used to be an engineer, he was telling me in the canteen. Aircraft and missiles and stuff. He did coding or something like that. Brilliant on computers apparently. He was made redundant twice after those defence cuts in the nineties and then became a warden as a temporary measure just to keep funds coming in for him and his missus to pay the mortgage. Just for a few months he reckoned, but you know the score. Ten years later and he's still here and going nowhere, and by the looks of things he's quite happy with it all."

"Ah well," replied Dan, "it were his own fault. Any rate, we could follow their example and if this terrorist threat comes to owt, perhaps we could hurl them at the suicide bombers. Right, here we are again. Get them cones out Dave and we can get down to the depot at last."

Dan's reverence for cones didn't extend to actually handling the things unless he had to. His duty was to drive the van, not put out cones. "Right, let's.....what the 'ell! Shit, look at that will yer. That bird's got virtually nowt on. Them tits, and look at her legs. Right up to her arse and then some! Hold on Dave. I'll come out an' 'elp yer with them bloody cones." He clambered hurriedly out of the driver's seat, grabbed a cone and moved swiftly round to the scene of the action, his eyes popping out of his head as the girl bent over to retrieve a dropped purse.

'I'll have to organise a few more of them' thought Dave, wonderingly. 'It's the first time I've ever seen Dan with a cone in his hand, and the first time I've seen him stand on his tongue. Or whatever it was.

"Fancy it a bit do you Dan? You old rogue. You'll be having affairs soon you know. It happens at your age. Anyway, she's only about sixteen and you never know, that could mean fourteen the way girls dress up nowadays. Twelve even!"

"She's never fourteen lad. I know fourteen year olds when I see them and no girl with tits and legs like that is fourteen, I can tell you. Anyway, look that's her boyfriend, and he's no boy."

"Probably her dad." Replied Dave, pushing the point.

"Oh sod off will yer."

It took a bit longer to put the cones out than normal as little could be done, until the girl had disappeared around the corner into Byron crescent, but eventually, with the cones safely out, it was time for that other urgent piece of morning Traffic Warden business - the tea break in the bus drivers' canteen. Passing the massed police cars parked along the double yellows near the canteen, Dave and Dan saw a very worried looking and fast moving Keith pushing rapidly through the canteen door. He stopped dead as Dan shouted to him.

"Oy! Keith! What's up? You're looking like you've got a dose of piles; probably from that cone up your arse the other day." Dan and Dave collapsed laughing as Keith's red face glared at them from the door.

"Go on laugh then. Have a good bloody laugh, but I'll have you know that our Reggie's been arrested as a terrorist. And not only that; they want to talk to all of us. Interrogate us! Decent Traffic Wardens as terrorists. I suppose that's what comes of associating with people like….."

"Hold on Keith," interrupted Dan. "Reggie, a terrorist? What the 'ell are you talking about?"

"It's true I tell you. Our Reggie. He's being interviewed by the police."

"Never!" responded Dan in amazement. "I could call Reggie a whole heap of things, most of 'em bad, but terrorist isn't one of 'em. Ow the 'ell has he got into this? Last thing I knew, people were trying to shoot him and he was trying to be a hero!"

"Well, he's down at the station now. A bloke came and got him in a plain clothed car. Just grabbed him and stuffed him in. Rough like! And they didn't look like proper cops to me. Bastards. That's what they looked like. Anyway, Barbara wants us all back in the crew room right away. You two get back there now and I'll grab the rest from the canteen. Shouldn't be in the bloody canteen this early anyway. Lazy sods."

"Shit," muttered Dan. "No breakfast. I was really looking forward to a number 4 with extra beans. Bloody Reggie! Them cones might come in handy after all!"

Once in the van, Dan recovered his equilibrium, as he always did when entering this haven from ordinary life. The van was his castle where he felt safe. No grotty members of the public, no hassle, everything familiar.

"I'm always happiest when I'm in the van you know Dave. Well, the canteen's OK as well of course, but then hearing about Reggie being a terrorist has put me off my breakfast now I come to think about it. I was thinking of a number 4 with extras, but I'm not sure I could stomach it now."

"D'you reckon he's one of those suicide people, you know those terrorist people who blow themselves up. He could be you know!"

"Course he isn't," replied Dan testily. You dull shit! Reggie, a suicide bomber! Are you trying to make me die laughing? Anyway, he hasn't blown anything up and if he had of done, according to your theory he'd be dead wouldn't he. Him being a suicide bomber I mean. Anyway, he likes being a hero too much. And you can't enjoy being a hero when you're dead."

Dave bowed to Dan's superior logic on this point and settled back in his seat. Dan was right, really. The van was indeed a sort of safe haven. Away from the world outside and anyway, he was glad that Reggie wasn't a suicide bomber. It wouldn't have been right.

The van and its occupants slowly made it from the canteen back to the station from where it had come just an hour before. Dan and Dave made their way through the back door of the station to the familiar and for a change, very overcrowded crew room where all the talk was about Reggie the terrorist.

Chapter Five

As he left the station, Reggie was not yet alarmed about matters connected to the robbery. He was still a hero, even if the rest of the Traffic Wardens refused to acknowledge it. He walked out of the police station with a spring in his step, fully expecting that the police or whoever it was from London wanted to consult him on beating robbers and gunmen at their own game. He decided he'd modestly play down the hero bit and just stick to the facts as he remembered them. Barbara had mentioned terrorists. Well, he wasn't too knowledgeable about them, but he was looking forward to putting his views forwards. He walked briskly towards the waiting car where Stan was holding a rear door open for him.

"Get in, keep quiet and behave yourself. OK?" Stan grabbed Reggie by the arm and pushed him roughly through the door. Reggie tumbled onto the back seat, furious that someone was treating him, a known hero, in such a manner.

Little did he know that compared to what was coming over the next few days, Stan's treatment of him would seem almost like a kindness!

Reggie didn't like the police. Even though he was now a Council Traffic Warden, the wardens used to be a Police operation and until a few years ago, he had a police badge on his jumper and was technically and actually a

Police Traffic Warden. The Police themselves, however? He taught them overbearing, over confident, swaggering oafs who would do better to get some proper traffic training in like in the old days. Mrs Elworthy's comment about him always pretending to be a copper just because he had once had a police badge had hurt and had aroused in him his usual feelings of total inadequacy when faced by a real policeman despite the fact that he knew they were oafs. And they weren't all that gentle getting him in that car, either! But this youngish, slightly balding, very well-dressed man sitting in DI Brightwell's temporary office claimed he wasn't a copper at all and indeed, to Reggie's practiced eye, he didn't look like one.

He greeted Reggie with outstretched arm and shook his hand heartily. "My dear chap," he smiled with a clipped Oxford accent. "My name's Smythe and you're the local hero and saviour of the postman. How are you now?" Without waiting for an answer, the man waved Reggie to a comfy chair and offered him a drink of coffee. By this time, Reggie was even more nervous. People didn't treat him like this usually. In fact never. But here was some important knob actually smiling and asking after his health and giving him coffee. And in a china cup.

"A bit better, thank you," he mumbled suspiciously. He sipped his coffee gingerly as though it might contain polonium, for some reason not daring to ask for milk or sugar.

The man nodded happily. "Now Reggie, my dear chap, I'm sorry the local DI isn't here. I did ask him to be but perhaps he had better things to do. Anyway, I'll come straight to the point. You may have something of ours." Reggie looked up.

"Something? What something do you mean officer?"

"Oh, I'm no officer Reggie. Let's just say I'm a civil servant. I work in London in a very minor capacity at the Home Office. Now about our property. It's a small envelope. A small package in fact. What's in it isn't that important, but the people whose property it is, are, and Her Majesty's Government would dearly like them to have it back. Now!" This last word spoken rather sharply thought Reggie.

Reggie still wasn't sure what he was talking about and for the life of him couldn't remember any package, but said, "what's it doing going by post then if it's that important. Why not by courier or in person like?"

"Ah Reggie" replied the man shaking his head. "I now have to reveal our best kept secret. It's actually safer to send really important stuff like diamonds, jewellery and important papers in the ordinary, anonymous post mixed in with millions of other packages and envelopes and flyers and so on. Indeed, as you may have heard on the news, the incident you got involved in was a diamond robbery. Unfortunately, our package was in the same bag.

No one takes any notice of the ordinary post. Courier vans always have valuables in them and are the first things to be attacked. The good old GPO Reggie. That's what we use. True, it didn't work this time, because of those diamonds that somebody knew about. Because of them, someone arranged for the little piece of action that you so bravely entered into. We aren't interested in those however. We want an entirely separate package that was also in that post bag. Now if you could give me the package, you'd be doing your country a fine service."

"I don't remember no package," mumbled Reggie worriedly. This was getting deep and he didn't like deep matters, especially if they included high up officials and services to country and stuff like that. In fact, he felt one of his turns coming on. And he really couldn't remember a package. And where was Dibsey? Barbara said he'd be here.

The man's smile became fixed as he looked carefully at Reggie.

"Now Reggie, old boy. We know you have it. The Police caught those bungling fools who robbed the van in a pub five minutes after they ran from you and your gun, and it wasn't in the bag. I haven't yet spoken to the dear lady herself, but one of the nurses told me that she saw a Mrs Elworthy, the only other witness to your 'heroism' in inverted commas, give it to you soon after you arrived in hospital and after you woke up. Mrs Elworthy told her that was what she was there to do, so you see Reggie. You have it somewhere, and we want it. What has happened is that the bang on the head that you so gallantly sustained must have had some small effect on your memory at the time, but not to worry, we perfectly understand that. Perfectly! But now of course we need to remind you about the matter and of course retrieve our property."

Reggie looked peeved. "Heroism! Why did you say it like that? In inverted commas? What the hell does that mean? Are you suggesting that I'm not a proper hero? I've got a wound you know and what's more……."

The man cut in soothingly. "Yes, yes, yes, Reggie. Of course you are a proper hero. And anyway, it doesn't matter what Mrs Elworthy or I think of you, the papers say you are a proper hero. It's all over town. Everyone knows about hero Reggie, so don't worry about that. Just tell me about the package."

"What package? I don't remember no package. I keep telling you, I don't know about any package. I don't know what that old bag Elworthy told you, but I don't remember no package." Reggie iterated his last four words carefully and slowly. He had seen someone in a film do it and it seemed to deflate the opposition. He looked up and smirked, confident that his power play would in turn deflate this overconfident although admittedly cultured git. But it didn't.

The git leaned in towards Reggie, accidentally nudging his coffee cup and depositing hot coffee over Reggie's groin. When his now very unsmiling face was less than an inch from a painfully grimacing Reggie's and his hand painfully squeezing Reggie's arm, he too iterated his words carefully.

"You do have it Reggie. I have now reminded you of the fact, so get me the package Reggie, or I'll have you arrested on terrorist charges. And, I'll make it stick. And you'll go down for years. And before you go down, a couple of friends of mine might just want to see you in a dark alley. There's more to this than you will ever know my friend." He gave Reggie's arm an extra painful squeeze and leaned back, smiling once again.

Reggie was outraged by this yobbo behaviour and he decided to make his views known straight away. "That'll bruise you know you bastard. That's wrongful abuse….and threats to my bodily person. And how can I go anywhere right now. I look as though I've pissed myself. That was bloody hot you know. I want a lawyer….."

"You'll get a lawyer Reggie. Just not yet because I think you are going to cooperate without one. And if you don't? Well, as I said, there are other ways to help you to decide to do what we want. Now I suggest you dry yourself off, go home, get that package and come straight back here with it. I'll give you an hour. And if you're not back then I'll come and get you. And you won't like that I can assure you."

Using a three year old copy of the 'Pig Breeder's Weekly' that he had found in the waiting room, to cover his groin area, Reggie stood up, left the office, slammed the door and walked hurriedly out of the police station, unbelievably relieved to get out of the presence of that dangerous bastard inside. Almost running down the entrance steps, he saw a fast moving and very annoyed looking Detective Inspector Brightwell, who in a rush to get in his car, didn't even notice him.

Dibsey had been called out to a hit and run incident involving a red Porsche on the other side of town. He could have done without that he told himself, but he reckoned he had plenty of time. The interview with Reggie with the bloke from London wasn't until 10.30. He'd get all this wrapped up in no time and get back to prepare things and have a chat with Percy from London. He was looking forward to having a yarn about the London scene and the big actions they had up there.

Percival Smythe sat back in his chair with a satisfied smile on his face. No point wasting petrol taking Reggie back to his dump of a house in the official car. Reggie had seemed sufficiently frightened to do as he was told. Composing his face, he waited for what he assumed would be an angry series of explosions from DI

Brightwell when he returned from his little, specially arranged hit and run diversion. He'd soon get that flash drive back After all, if the Home Secretary wanted it back, he, Percy would get it back. Of interest to the Prime Minister himself, he'd been told and failure to retrieve it could have horrendous consequences for the Government and the country.

Reggie in the meantime was moving fast. "They're all bastards," he mumbled as he moved swiftly down the street towards an urgently needed pint at the Pig and Whistle. It was a bit early and maybe Deidre wouldn't serve him, but as he looked in through the window, he saw her cleaning up from the night before, and she beckoned him in with a cheery wave. He sat at a table near the bar and ordered his first pint.

Strange that bastard Brightwell wasn't at the interview, he thought as he threw the pint down. He usually gets his nose stuck into any trough that's going, especially if it's people from London. He thought he'd better phone in and say he'd be a bit late, but didn't want to speak to Barbara about it, so pulling out his Traffic Warden mobile number list; he dialled up Dave and left a message. Dave was OK; one of the better sorts of Traffic Warden. He'd pass it on OK. He fumbled with the knobs and turned his radio emphatically 'off' and sat and sank his second pint without even noticing it and wondered what the hell he was going to do about the package business. Old Bag Elworthy he thought when well into his third. I'll go and see her as soon as I get out of here. She seems to know something about the bloody package. He called out to Deidre at the bar for a fourth and decided not to go back in that day at all.

Chapter Six

Dan and Dave arrived much later than they had wanted to at the meeting called over the new development of Reggie's terrorist activity, and had to shoulder their way through the throng of on and off duty Traffic Wardens crowding the crew room. Word had spread swiftly that something different was going on. They had had to stop on the way in and ticket a bright red Porsche that had parked itself right across the entrance to a residential property driveway and the irate property owner, who wanted to get off to work had berated them for a full twenty minutes for not being immediately to hand when this criminal deed was committed. As they were finally able to drive away from the scene, they saw the Porsche drive off, the driver hurling pieces of ticket out of the window as he drove. They also passed DI Brightwell hurtling down the main express route through town apparently following the same red Porsche.

As soon as Barbara entered the room, the hubbub died away to a mere whisper, everyone anxious to hear the full details of Reggie's latest folly. Terrorism was new to Traffic Warden sensibilities and any announcement on the subject would immediately enter the hallowed book of Traffic Warden folklore. It would be something to talk about for many years to come and if you could say you were actually there, at the scene, at the actual meeting on the day, and therefore associated with it, in however minor a way; then you would be able to command any conversation on the subject for years to come in crew rooms and pubs across the country.

Barbara looked carefully around the room before speaking and her first words took everyone by surprise.

"Has anyone actually seen Reggie since the morning briefing?" Everyone in the room looked at each other, shaking their heads and a chorus of noes echoed around the room. "Because he went down to the police station an hour or more ago in an unmarked police car for an interview about certain events, and I've just had a call from Dibsey to say that he wants to see him again. Urgently or he'll be in more trouble than ever. Needless to say, Dibs is in one of his totally out of control, arsehole moods and even had the nerve to accuse Traffic Wardens of being unable to organise a piss-up in a brewery and has threatened to shoot Reggie on sight when he sees him."

The room erupted. This was fighting talk and no one, especially the police and even more especially Detective Inspector bloody Bright-bloody-well had any right to even breathe the same air as Traffic Wardens let alone slag them off and even worse, threaten, however much in jest, to shoot one. Even if it was Reggie! The mood in the room subtly changed after Barbara said that. No longer were the team looking to find fun in the Reggie terrorist/hero situation. Reggie was a colleague. Another Traffic Warden with the Traffic Warden Tango Whisky call sign. Out there daily facing people who couldn't even comprehend the importance of police cones! OK, he was a bit odd at times, but who wasn't. Reggie needed support and they were the ones to give it. Dan looked at Dave and shook his head slowly.

"Ee! Now there'll be trouble. That copper ad no right to say that. Reggie's probably gone home. I mean, e's a lot of things, most of them bloody odd, but e's no terrorist is 'e."

Conversations began to get more heated, but before the room erupted into all out declarations of war, Barbara raised her hand. Despite Dibsey's provocation, she had a duty to ensure harmonious relations between the police who were her main stakeholder, this group of oddballs in front of her who were technically her charges. Deciding not to sit down due to her rampant pile situation, she carefully brought everyone in the room up to date on the Reggie situation which actually wasn't very much. The main purpose of talking to them however was to stop uninformed gossip from getting out of hand. She knew that this lot were experts at it and if left unchecked, rumours of who knows what would be spreading around the town at warp speed.

"Anyway," she shouted above the noise. The first thing to do is to find out where Reggie has disappeared off to. Oh, and contrary to what you may have heard, they don't want to interview everyone. Just Reggie. Now then, he's not answering his radio and his mobile's probably out of juice. Dan and Dave, take the cone van round to his place and keep knocking on the door until someone answers. His old mum's as deaf as a coot. After that take a look around the area and then continue with the cone jobs. Jan, you take Reggie's area 5 and see if he just went back to work. Take a peek into the Royal. I know it's early but the pubs open early these days for coffees, and most of them will serve a pint if asked, especially to regulars. Polly, take a look in the Pig. He might just have decided that he's had enough and gone for a pint in his old favourite. I hope not at this hour, but you never know. Henrietta, you go with her. You know what Deidre at the Pig is like. Anyone, anytime is her motto. As for the rest of you; go about your normal duties in your areas and just keep an eye out for the sod. OK! Go!"

The room turned as one for the door and Barbara walked painfully back to her office and sat down heavily onto her rubber ring cushion, her right hand sliding deftly towards her lower cabinet draw. Right from the start, she'd had that strange feeling that the Reggie business was going to run on and on and now she was certain. She had seen Reggie get in that unmarked police car and so she couldn't understand why he hadn't arrived back. Just a small chat that posh bloke had said. And where was the stupid bugger now? Her life would be so simple, if people like Reggie simply didn't exist. But she knew down deep that he was one of theirs, certainly no terrorist and it appeared he was going to need all of their support. And anyway, Dan and Dave would sort it out round at Reggie's house. Or rather his old mum's house. That's where she reckoned he'd be. Reggie hadn't quite made that move in life yet.

Idly thinking of terrorists, she took a double take when Boobs Durrani, her favourite Welsh Pakistani poked his head round the door. "Oh Boobs, you're late. Can you check out the canteen please and see if Reggie is there. He's not answering his radio or mobile and we need to find him quickly. He often pops in there thinking I don't know about it."

Boobs, actually Mahboob Durrani, a wannabe leading light in the town theatre club, grinned with delight. The canteen was also his favourite place as well despite some of the more obnoxious English breakfasts served there. 'These Traffic Wardens,' he thought to himself. 'A wonderful crew. Each year they come and see me in a production at the old playhouse.' Each year he played a variety of parts, and played them well. He had often thought of giving up his day job and becoming an actor of stage and screen, but each time he gathered his nerve for the move, a new bill arrived to slap him round the head and remind him that he needed a regular job, now, not in the future. His wife was also fairly forceful in that regard too. The stage was his fantasy life. New, and very expensive rip off school uniforms for the kids, rip off rates, the mortgage and the rip off prices at the supermarket were reality.

"Boobs, you're daydreaming! We've really got to find Reggie before anyone else does and find out exactly what is going on. I've got a strange feeling that things are going to go from bad to worse if the police get to him first, especially if it's those London blokes whoever they are. Apparently, they are after him. Now get on with it."

She sat back to take the weight off her piles and watched Boobs scoot off on his mission, and hoped for the best. Things were getting weird and she didn't like weird.

Chapter Seven

It was half way through pint five when a tiny but persistent thought managed to intrude itself into Reggie's befuddled mind and he jolted upright as he suddenly remembered what he was meant to be doing. He looked wildly around for a few seconds and mumbled to Deidre that he needed to go for a piss.

"I don't need to know that Reggie, thank you," she said primly. "Just let me know when you want another pint and in the meantime, do what you have to do."

Suddenly desperate, Reggie shot into the gents and leaned over the urinal, his outstretched arm holding himself off the wall and his head hanging down watching the seemingly endless stream disappearing down the loo pipe. 'Come on, come on; bloody hurry up,' he mumbled at his dick, and what seemed like hours later, he swiftly managed to fumble his flies up. Grabbing the copy of the Pig Breeder's weekly off his table and again covering his groin area due to the speed with which he'd had to finish his ablutions causing a series of major dribbles, he rushed from the pub, leaving, to Deidre's astonishment, some of pint number five still in his glass on the table.

The sheer weight of beer swilling around in his body nearly toppled Reggie over several times as he wobbled up Knightsbank parade towards the underpass and he looked around worriedly as he approached the scene of the robbery. Stopping quickly and furtively to add to the smell of urine in the darkest part of the underpass, he weaved his way towards Shelley Mansions, the ugly and rather seedy block of flats further up the street, one of which housed Mrs Elworthy. To cover a whole new area of dribbles and damp patches on his trousers he pulled a few sheets out of the Pig Breeder and held them in two hands. Soon need a whole bloody newspaper to wrap up in at this rate, he thought worriedly and was glad to see Shelley Mansions closing swiftly. Reggie knew she was in when he saw her red Lada sitting out on the road next to the curb. She never went anywhere without her car, or Muggins. Ugly little sod thought Reggie as he stumbled through the gate. 'One of those dogs with a pushed in face and bulgy eyes. Can't stand them.'

As he clumped up the stairs, a new thought entered Reggie's beer befuddled brain. What if the old bag wouldn't play? She was never one to be cooperative in anything and at best was totally unpredictable. He well remembered the time she drove off a two hour slot less than a minute before he could slap a ticket on her windscreen. He'd even got as far as writing the bloody thing out in anticipation of a major coup against the old bat and because of that he'd had to write out a detailed report explaining why he shouldn't be accused of favouring Mrs Elworthy in a corruption charge. He still couldn't work out how she had managed to surprise him like that. It was a though she had shot up out of the ground right next to him, got in the car and driven off. She hadn't even looked at him and for a long while he truly thought that she might be a witch of some sort and that the hideous looking Muggins was her familiar. He peered at each door looking for her name and finally found it on the third floor, number seven. None of the other doors seemed to have names on them. "Bout bloody time, " he mumbled to himself, desperate for another piss.

Anticipating trouble, he straightened up in the hope of making some sort of impression on her and leant wearily against the door. Emboldened by 4 and three quarter pints of the Pig's finest bitter he boldly hammered his right fist on her door, just as Mrs Elworthy opened it. His fist hit on nothing, and aided by an enormous, surprise fart, Reggie toppled forward, straight past her and hit the floor with a thud, as Muggins, yapping furiously, flew in to the attack.

Reggie came to slowly. He was a mass of pain all over if he moved, and he couldn't work out where he was or what had happened, or even if he was still alive, and he didn't want to open his eyes to find out. He somehow knew instinctively that if he did, he would not like what he saw; and he was right. Finally, unable to deny the fact that he was still alive, he opened his right eye and shrieked aloud at the terrifying sight of Muggins's nostrils and bulging eyes literally a millimetre from his own. Believing from Reggie's shriek and noise that another attack was perfectly in order, Muggins launched at Reggie's face before being hauled off, just in time, by a fast moving Mrs Elworthy.

"Ah, you're awake are you, Mr Traffic Warden? About time I must say. I was about to call either an ambulance or someone from your office to come and get you. Lying around on my sofa indeed!"

Reggie looked down and found himself lying on a threadbare and very lumpy sofa, under an equally threadbare brown blanket. And to his horror, he didn't have any trousers on. In a sudden panic, he quickly felt down under the blanket, imagining all sorts of weird scenarios, including having been kidnapped by a sex maniac, but his huge relief, his underpants were safe and sound and still on, if a bit damp, and his movements only brought on sharp pains all over his legs. He looked quickly under the blanket and saw plasters all over his bare legs. Where the hell had they come from? His world was getting weirder by the minute and Reggie was beginning to wonder after all if he was still in the land of the living, or in some sort of hell. He whipped around again, wincing in pain as Mrs Elworthy suddenly spoke from behind him.

"Had to get them off you. They were ripped to pieces, your trousers were." Her voice went all silly and babyish. "Little Muggins - ah, there's a good little boysie woisie," She bent down to pat his ugly, bulgy eyed head and smiled fondly. "Little Mugsy Wugsy thought nasty Traffic Warden was attacking mumsy wumsy didn't you. Oh, he's such a handsome boy." She tickled his chin as his bulging eyes looked up at her adoringly. "You can't blame him, can you? It's his territory after all. He was protecting me. I'll sew them up a bit to make up. In the meantime you can wear Mr Elworthy's trousers. They've seen no use since the old boy died years ago, God rot his frosty faced soul. Might be a bit big mind. Short, he was, but wide in the beam as it were. I've put plasters and Dettol on the bites where the skin's broke. He nearly got you right in the whatsits didn't he? My word, you were dead lucky there Mr Traffic Warden. Just a scratch on it. Anyway, what are you doing here and why was your trousers all damp. Is it raining out there?"

"Yes, raining," mumbled Reggie quickly, anxiously looking under the blanket at his wounded privates and eager to avoid talk of his wet trousers.

"Want a cuppa then?" asked Mrs Elworthy, looking him over. "Might as well wait until I've sorted them trousers out."

"Got anything stronger," asked Reggie, more in hope than expectation.

"Might have," she replied and disappeared off to the small kitchen down the passage. To Reggie's amazement, she returned with what looked suspiciously like a litre bottle of whisky and then to his further astonishment pushed a shot glass brimming with the golden elixir into his hand.

"Get this down then and I might just have one with you, and I think you've got some explaining to do. Now then get it out."

Reggie looked up in alarm before realising that she just wanted him to speak about why he was at her flat, and with the whisky reinforcing the beneficial effects of the Pig's best bitter, he explained what had happened so far and the fact that he had to get back within one hour with the package to give it to a representative of the country's authorities.

"An hour! Well, you've had that, haven't you? Anyway, what authorities?" sneered Mrs Elworthy when Reggie finally ground to a halt. Mrs Elworthy was not one for authorities. Morons; the lot of them she always thought. Especially Traffic Wardens, but anyway. She poured another whisky for each of them and carried on.

"From what you say, how do you know the man was an official? This bloke whom interviewed you. Did he offer any ID? No. Was Dibsey there? No. Is that likely? No. A lot of negatives aren't there? I haven't got the package anyway. I gave it to you in the hospital like the man said. You were lying there all dozy like, just like today, and I left it on your bedside table. At least I assume that's the package they mean. Small brown package? Almost like an envelope? Fell in a puddle. Too wet to see any name or address on it?"

Reggie nodded, recognising the description afforded by Percy.

"Well, don't you go giving anything to anyone? Strange men from London who aren't cops don't interview Traffic Wardens without the local cop there and they don't threaten people with violence when they do interview them unless they're not recording - and nowadays they have to record. Simple. Now, you go back home and search all the usual places for that packet of whatever. You'll have put it somewhere. Don't be seen and then you get back here…."

She stopped suddenly and thought. "In fact, better still, I'll drive you there. They don't know my Lada from Adam and so they won't notice it. Somehow Mr Traffic Warden, you've dropped yourself right in it and I reckon you're going to need me around to sort you out. I don't like officials or robbers and the like so on that basis I'll help you. Now then, Reggie Parkes, I suggest you get a move on."

"Yes, OK," mumbled Reggie in surprise. Was this the Mrs Elworthy he thought she was, he asked himself silently? This Mrs Elworthy was positive and assured and seemed to know what she was talking about; a world away from the moaning old bag in the underpass. This Mrs

Elworthy seemed like someone he could do business with. Someone he could rely on. He brightened; someone who could take charge. And hero or no hero,that is desperately what he wanted someone to do.

"Well, I'm Phyllis," she replied and Reggie mumbled his approval as she splashed another couple of whiskies into the generously sized shot glasses, one of which he gratefully drank while she went off to the bedroom to fetch dead Mr Elworthy's trousers.

Phyllis, eh? Slurred Reggie. "I like that name."

Chapter Eight

Percy Smith - the 'y' and the 'e' dropped now that he was alone and with no need to impress anyone, was becoming a touch worried. Few matters worried him generally, but that idiot Traffic Warden had been gone far more than an hour now, more like two hours and he wished he had told Stan, his minder and driver, to take him straight to his house, or wherever he lived and help him look for the package. Stan would have brooked no nonsense. He'd have hauled Reggie into the house, kicked his arse until he found the thing, taken hold of it, kicked Reggie about a bit to remind him who's who, and walked out. He thought he had scared Reggie sufficiently to make him obey his instructions without delay, but obviously something had gone astray, or the stupid arse had got himself run over. He should also have spoken to Mrs Elworthy as well, but what the hell, you can't do everything on your own, he thought angrily. His masters however, did want everything done on his own, and yesterday at that, which was why Percy was beginning to get worried. And he did want Reggie back in the station when that fool Brightwell turned up. And Reggie was patently not there. It was with great effort that he straightened up and smiled as DI Brightwell bounded into the office, hand outstretched in welcome.

"Glad to see you here again Mr Smythe. I'd have been here earlier, but got called out on some fool's errand. I'm going to have to have a word with dispatch. Silly buggers! All it was, was a parking incident. Anyway, Reggie Parkes should be here soon and we can get on and interrogate the bastard. I'm not one for Traffic Wardens…"

Percy cut in quickly. He recognised DI Brightwell as one of those over friendly, 'let's all be pals cos we're all on the same side' coppers who do nothing but talk and drink in the police bar.

"He's been and gone detective. I did say 8 a.m. and you weren't here, so I interviewed him myself. The desk Sergeant let me in and showed me the office. Thanks for that by the way. Shoddy work, not being here as agreed though, but I've got to make a move now. I sent Reggie home to pick up a package for us and he hasn't returned yet so it seems I must go and get him and it won't be pleasant. Bye now Inspector."

"But you said 10.30" gasped Dibsey in confusion. "I'm sure you said 10.30 and it's only 10.15 now." He now looked flustered and upset. DI Brightwell was a keen guardian of his turf and if something was going on in it; he should be the first to know about it. He rarely did, but that wasn't the point. Strange London people interviewing suspects on his patch without him being around was totally out of order. "You'd better………"

But Percy had upped and gone. Striding past Dibsey, he walked straight out of the station, flicked his fingers at Stan, waited the three seconds until his car coasted up to him, got in and disappeared.

"Bastard!" gasped Dibsey in disbelief at his treatment. "Bloody, sodding bastard! Who the hell does he think he is?" He spluttered to a halt, completely unable to think of anything else to say. And finally, as he began his deep breathing exercises, recommended by his GP, Doctor Aahlaadita Chattopadhyay, his mind began to advance from slow snail speed to racing snail speed, and he turned from the steps of the police station and went slowly back to his office and thinking deeply about the lovely Aahlaadita, he equally slowly, picked up the phone. But once on it, his mind roared into action. As did his mouth.

He dialled rapidly and roared down the phone. "Barbara, is Reggie there? If he is, I want to see him now."

"Well you can't. He's not here and in fact, since those mates of yours took him off, we haven't seen him. Could have gone home for all I know. But I've got a van going round there after a couple of tasks and they'll bring him in. Leave it to us."

"Well he'll be in total shit when I get hold of the bastard, I can tell you that for free. I'll personally shoot the sod. I'll lock him up Barbara, I tell you." Dibsey slammed the phone down and looked up Reggie's address on the electronic index. Northbrook Road. "Right," he mumbled, "better get to him before that bastard Smythe does and before that Traffic Warden van. I'll never know what's going on unless I do and the Chief Super will kill me." He picked up the phone again.

"Brightwell here," he shouted down the phone, "Get a car round here straight away. I need to get to 39 Northbrook Road pronto! Yes, I know it just went in. Well, I want it to come back out. NOW!" 'No bastard's going to piss me around' he mumbled as he left the office. 'Bastard Smythe, thinks he can take Dibsey on. Well bastard Smythe has another think coming. Dibsey walked hurriedly to the station front door and waited impatiently on the steps for the car to turn up. "Where's that sodding car? Ah."

Dibsey had the door open even before the car had stopped; leaped in, mumbled something at the driver while his mind twisted and turned over the bastard who had dared speak to him like that in his own office, waved half-heartedly to a police Sergeant standing at the curb waving to him for some reason, and as the car rocketed off he slowly shut his eyes, to try and fend off the approaching migraine. 'It's not far he thought as his eyes began to close. We'll be there in no time and I can sort it all out. I'll pick up Reggie, haul him back here and put him in a cell for a while until everything is sorted. Safer that way, otherwise thing can get out of hand. I just need to get to him fast. And I don't want that Smythe bastard anywhere near him this time.' His head lowered itself slowly into his chest and he swiftly dozed off.

"Straight to Reggie's house Stan," said Percy. "I think we need a bit of direct action around here or the boss will have our privates." The car took of smoothly down Lancashire Avenue. "39 Northbrook Road. Can you get there?" Stan looked round at his boss and smiled. He hadn't been a cabbie for nothing. He knew every inch of every road around here and had swindled more customers than anyone else in town by taking long cuts full of traffic lights. His eventual disbarment from cabbydom had done much to improve both the satisfaction level of taxi users and the rate of Stan's progress through life and when he had been offered a job through a mate of a mate who knew a mate of a cousin, Stan had met Percy and had prospered.

"As soon as we get there Stan, just walk in, grab that bastard Reggie if he's there, ask him nicely to get the package and bring him out and stuff him in the car. There's a few more things I'd like to ask him about. And I don't mean to be pleasant."

Stan nodded happily. "OK Boss. We'll be there in no time."

Phyllis revved up her Lada. "We'll get you to your mum's house quick like Reggie, and you can go in and get the packet and then tell her to lock the door fast. We don't want those other buggers poking around." Reggie, nodded in agreement, happy to be doing something in the company of this woman.

"Where do you live anyway?" Phyllis looked sideways at a worried looking Reggie, wondering if he had the balls to do this quickly and efficiently, as she would have done.

"Northbrook Road. 39. it's just off the park, not far from the railway station. About 15 minutes."

She decided Reggie would be OK and accelerated hard, heading for Northbrook Road. "Don't worry Reggie," she said calmly, "We'll get this thing sorted out. Just get the packet, and we'll decide what to do with it then. And don't worry; we'll be there in no time." Something about the way he seemed so vulnerable appealed to her. And he looked after his old mum. Strange, she thought because she had never liked Traffic Wardens before. And another thought; it was a chance for her to take charge of someone which she could never do when old Mr Elworthy ruled the roost.

Reggie's disappearance was at that very moment exercising the minds of most of the Traffic Wardens. It still wasn't a critical absence, but it was beginning to seem strange, particularly due to the involvement of that strange cop and the message that Reggie had left on Dave's mobile phone. It said 'Dave, it's Reggie. Won't be coming in today. Those London blokes are after me.' Dave had told Barbara, which just added to her puzzlement and anxiety.

"We'll just get these bloody cones in and then call up Keith and then we can get off to see where the 'ell Reggie disappeared to, OK Dave?"

"Yeah, fine, in fact that's the last of them Dan. Are you going to do lights and siren?" Dave always used the cone van's lights and siren when he was driving. He could, cross red lights and generally disobey rules. But Dan was more cautious. He had once suffered the indignity of being overtaken by a car load of grinning, finger waving yobs while he had his lights and sirens going.

"No, we don't want to do that. The van can't go fast enough and we'll look right prats racing along at 40 with all our bells and whistles going and everyone else held up behind us. We'll get there in our own time Dave. Where does Reggie live anyway?"

"Tango Whisky 46, repeat Tango Whisky 46," radioed Dave. "Eh, Barbara; where's Reggie's house then? Over."

"007 to Tango Whisky 46, Northbrook Road; 39. Keep to police radio protocols, Dave, no names on the radio. You should know that. Is Keith with you yet, and if you see Jan and Henrietta, take them as well. They want to help out as Reggie seems to be in trouble? Over."

"Not got Keith yet, we're on our way to pick him up now. Roger and out. Got that Dan? Northbrook Road. We can cut up Chancellor Street, cross by the park and hit that big road that leads onto Northbrook. Once we've got Keith, we'll be there in no time." He wished his call sign was 007. He would have died for it.

They rounded the corner and there was Keith looking as agitated as ever and arguing with a couple of real nasty looking pieces of work with shaved heads, nose rings and a clapped out Cortina. He looked highly relieved as he saw the van approach.

"C'mon Keith, get in," rasped Dan through the window. Even before the van had stopped, Keith had grabbed the handle and wrenched the door open and leapt in, landing straight onto Dave.

"No, not here, in the back," shouted Dave.

"I'm senior here and I'm not going in the back. You go in the back," shouted Keith.

"I'm on van duty," retorted Dave. "I'm not going in the back. This is my place. My place of duty. So piss off Keith. This seat's too small for three."

"Well, you can bloody well sit in the middle, then with the hand brake sticking up your arse for all I care," said Keith. "Now you piss off, cos I'm not moving." He sat there on Dave's lap, gripping the seat edge in order to secure his place.

"And neither am I," shouted Dave. "This is my place, so get in there with those bloody cones. And who said you're senior anyway." He pushed Keith hard sideways to dislodge him from his lap but instead knocked him right across Dan causing him to knock his head hard against the side window glass and to drive the van directly towards the main front door and windows of the Pig and Whistle.

"Keith for fu………" But Dan didn't manage to finish his sentence, because as he wrenched the wheel round to try and recover the straight and narrow path of the van and avoid hitting the pub, his hand slipped in the sweaty panic of the situation and in a shower of glass, from windows and beer bottles, accompanied by smashing, screeching, banging and tearing sounds, Dan finally lodged what remained of the nose of the van into the splintered, finely veneered planking of the main bar of the Pig and Whistle.

"Well that's a neat bit of parking," railed Keith sarcastically, brushing pieces of window glass off his shoulder. "Reggie would've been real proud of that one. Right up to the bar of the Pig. Wonderful! We can all have a drink now. There's sod all else to do, is there cos we can't go anywhere. And you can bloody well buy the round Dave!"

Deidre's head slowly rose from behind the bar, her look of horror turning to amazement as she saw the three Traffic Wardens sitting in the front seat of the van, looking at her from just a couple of feet away. Keith was sitting on Dave's lap for some reason.

"Reggie left half an hour ago," she heard herself say slowly. "If that's who you're after. He left some of his pint. It was his fifth. It's over there."

The heads of the three Traffic Wardens slowly followed Deirdre's as she turned and pointed at Reggie's unfinished pint. They all snapped back to normality as Dan's radio burst loudly into life.

"Tango Whisky 46. Tango Whisky 46." Barbara's voice blared over the airwaves. "Dan? Have you picked up Keith yet? Is that a police siren I hear ………?"

Dan turned and grabbed his radio. "Oh fuck off Barbara will yer. We're a bit busy right now. 46 Out."

Chapter Nine

"What the bloody hell was that?" exclaimed Polly as she and Henrietta rounded the corner into Ranfurley Street. "Henrietta, quick, come here. Someone's just crashed into the Pig. I think!" They surveyed the rubble and wreckage of the front of the pub.

"Oh dear!" said Henrietta, unsure for a few seconds of what else to say, and then recovered. "My Bill wouldn't drive right into the Pig. Ooh, Look! The whole front of the pub is all smashed in. There's bricks and glass everywhere. Look Polly! Is that our cone van in there? Up at the bar? My Bill's most insistent on parking several streets away. You know how the police hang around the pubs near closing to catch drunk drivers. Not that my Bill would........"

"Henrietta, for God's sake shut up drivelling will you. And yes, it is the bloody cone van. Shitty death! Look at it! What a mess. And there's Dan, Dave and Keith - and Deidre! How the hell did all this happen?"

The arrival of a small crowd of very interested, chattering bystanders, closely followed by two police cars and an ambulance brought an air of total unreality to the scene of devastation, with one elderly lady relating stories of the blitz to anyone who would listen. Dan, Dave and Keith were given a thorough once over by the paramedics and Deidre, on the verge of having a fit of the vapours was taken off by the ambulance crew to calm down and recover in hospital.

Polly and Henrietta in the meantime slipped away as fast as they were able to and headed straight back to the office to report matters to Barbara. They didn't dare say anything over the radio. Dan, Dave and Keith being miraculously, totally uninjured and seemingly still of sound mind, were taken to the police station for questioning. When they explained that the accident was as a result of their search for Reggie, all concern by the police interviewer for the state of the Pig and Whistle evaporated and they were told to wait for Detective Inspector Dibswell, who would take over the investigation from then on.

"He won't be long gentlemen," explained the desk sergeant. "I've seen him around this morning, so just make yourselves comfortable and I'll go and look him up."

The three sat down on the hard, plastic chairs provided for members of the public and stared gloomily at the standard green paint on the walls; none of them at all happy about being talked at by Dibsey.

"I hope the bastard turns up quick," muttered Dan worriedly. I wonder why he's going to talk to us. Normally they'd just take a few statements and let us go. Oh well; I suppose Dibsey'll enlighten us. It's all bloody Reggie's fault of course. Oh shit! Look who's 'ere."

"I send you two out on a simple errand. Look for Reggie, I said. Go to his mum's house. That's all I wanted you to do, and what happens. You pick up Keith and then go and park up at the bar of the Pig, having smashed down the front wall of the place with the van in your eagerness to get there, and then you tell me to fuck off over the radio so every bastard policeman in Westbourne, plus police central can hear you. They're all pissing themselves laughing now; those that can still stand up straight that is!"

Barbara groaned as an outbreak of the painfully itchy herpes spots on her backside added to increasing pain of her piles. "Well I'm going to leave you to stew in it here until Dibsey gets in and you can sort your story out between yourselves. You can bloody well sort it out with him as well. I've got to go and explain it to the Chief Super this afternoon, so get the story right and get it good. I'll speak to you buggers later on. And don't think for one second that this is anywhere near the end of the matter."

As elegantly as she was able, bearing in mind the open warfare between piles and herpes spots spreading across her backside, Barbara turned and stalked wearily out of the station. Her initial briefing for that day was fast unravelling, but so bloody what? She'd send Polly and Henrietta in the spare cone van round to Reggie's immediately to try and locate the so-called hero and bring him in, and she'd give an interim briefing on the day's events to the Police Chief Superintendent who usually took ownership of these types of matter as soon as she could order her thoughts. And that wasn't going to be easy. First though, she'd better find out the state of things with Reggie from that idiot Brightwell.

Dibsey, sitting back restfully in the plush seat of the car woke up with a start, hearing a vaguely familiar voice addressing him.

"Oh Inspector Brightwell! How nice of you to come along on this sad occasion. I'm so glad the police were able to send a representative, and an inspector at that. We are so pleased. Now come along please Inspector, I'll escort you into the church."

Dibsey started violently and looked around in alarm at the very unfamiliar scenery outside of the car. "Where the bloody hell have you taken me?" he hissed at the driver. "Is that a church? I wanted Northbrook Road you idiot. Where's this."

"This car was ordered to take a police representative to old Sergeant Bonniface's funeral sir in Weymouth. When you leaped in, I naturally thought you were that representative, and I resent being called an idiot, even by you sir."

The driver sniffed and faced the front as Dibsey began to launch another attack.

"Weymouth? We're in Weymouth? That's bloody miles away. Hour and a half at least. We've got to get back…Fuck….ah, excuse my French Vicar." The Vicar's head loomed again in the car window.

"We'd better get our seats in the church now if you don't mind now Inspector," said the Vicar, holding open the car door and obliging Dibsey to get out and follow him to the church.

"Now Vicar, as you can appreciate I've got a busy day today, catching criminals and so on," said Dibsey with a forced smile. "So if you……."

"Of course my dear boy. Of course. Of course, of course! The ceremony won't take long at all," replied the Vicar with a knowing smile. "But naturally a few words from your august self will be needed - not more than twenty minutes if you don't mind, but I'm sure you're prepared for that. And then we have a small gathering for a sherry and some cake afterwards, and old Mrs Bonniface will be so excited to have a chat with you personally. An Inspector no less! She misses the force more than her dear departed husband you know. She'll be so happy to see you. She'll no doubt have a lot of questions about how the force is getting on now."

They entered into the gloom of the church. "Anyway, here we are Inspector. Take a seat here and we can get this show on the road as you policemen would say. It's so nice you could come."

Dibsey sat down wearily at the end of the pew, vowing, in a most unchristian manner, to personally emasculate everyone involved in the car pool as well as Reggie Parkes and most of all Percival bloody Smythe, the bastard who had shat on his entire day. He turned his mind to thinking up the 'few words' he would have to say on behalf of the dear departed sergeant who he had never met or known, or even bloody well heard of until a minute ago. He was still wondering what on earth he was going to say when Barbara's text asking him where the hell he was came through.

The Vicar, still beaming at his congregation that now included a police inspector, began the ceremony to farewell retired Sergeant Henry Oliver Bonniface, policeman, war hero, retired, and much loved husband and father, most recently departed from this world.

"Hold it," hissed Reggie loudly as they rounded the corner into Northbrook Road. "That's the car that bastard Smythe at the police station was using. I never forget a number plate. And there, that's him and his moron of a sidekick going up to the door of mum's place. And look! He's parked on a double yellow. Bastard! What the hell do we do now?"

"'How's your mum in a spot Reggie?" asked Phyllis pulling over to the side of the road across from the house. "Can she cope with those two, as there's no point you going in there at the moment, but I do reckon you should ticket their car and maybe see if there's enough air in their tyres."

Reggie cottoned on to the plan immediately. Of course; he thought. A ticket! That's just what's needed. And a careful look at their tyres. "Excellent idea Phyllis. And as for mum, she doesn't believe anything anyone tells her even if she can hear what they said in the first place. She'll be OK."

As Stan's scream suddenly rent the air and echoed down Northbrook Road, Reggie smiled. "In fact, come to think of it Phyllis, those two bastards haven't got a clue about what they've let themselves in for."

Chapter Ten

Northbrooke Road was a pleasant street and according the works signs set up all over the place, it had been earmarked for improvement by the local council. Both the houses adjacent to Reggie's were empty, awaiting double glazing, new plumbing and electrics and insulation, but the gardens were still neat and tidy. The only blot on the landscape was the huge electrical transfer station just up the road, which provided current for most of the city and which tended to dominate the whole area, but most of the residents had long ago dismissed it as just one of those things and the area was still very much in demand.

"Ok Stan, let's get this over with," muttered Percy as they strode up the path towards Reggie's front door "I want out of this bloody town by lunchtime. If our hero Reggie's here we give him twenty seconds of nice guy act and then get down to business and if it's just his mum, we play the nice guys and if necessary I'll explain that we can get a warrant within ten minutes to search Reggie's belongings and warn her that it's in Reggie's interest that we find that bloody envelope. Don't worry, she'll play ball."

Reggie's mum was small, and she had a thin waspish face surmounted by short grey, wiry hair, closely resembling one of those wire wool scrubbing pads. In response to increasing louder knocks on the door which she could hear better only after inserting one of her hearing aids, she opened the front door to the extent of its sturdy chain and peered up at Percy and Stan.

"We've already got some," she shouted through the gap. "And we don't want no more, so piss off!"

"What the hell's the old coot talking about" snarled Stan, looking down at Mrs Parkes.

"Stan, just get ready to may be add a little force to the door when I say go. Probably won't be necessary but just in case. We do need that envelope." Stan put his hand round the door opening, just as a precaution, ready to muscle in and break the chain if required.

Percy smiled down and putting on his most reasonable voice, explained that they were Reggie's mates from work and they'd called round to collect an envelope for Reggie. He'd left it behind and now couldn't get off work.

"Oh, the envelope," said Mrs Parkes, still glaring at Stan. "Why didn't you say so? Wait a moment." She trotted off and returned less than minute later with a small brown package. "Is this it?"

"Thank you dear lady," said Percy, enormously relieved and firmly grabbing the small package quickly before she changed her mind. "Well, we'll take that and we'll be sure to pass it on to Reggie. Now you have a really nice day."

"I will, now piss off," shouted Reggie's mum and slammed the heavy door hard against Stan's fingers.

The scream could be heard right up the street and beyond and Reggie grinned at Phyllis as he watched the scene unfolding. Stan was making a hell of a racket with his hand stuck in the door and Percy hopping around on the steps, unable to decide whether to leave Stan to his fate or try and get him released.

"Open the door." Screamed Stan again. "Open the effing door. My fingers are broken. Open the door. Mrs Parkes, please open the door." Tear streamed down Stan's cheeks as he struggled vainly to extricate his hand from the door.

The door opened. "I told you to piss off didn't I? Don't tell me about vacuum cleaner bags. I know all about vacuum cleaner bags. My Reggie knows all about vacuum cleaner bags……"

But Stan was no longer there. Clutching his right hand which had fingers sticking out in all directions, and whimpering loudly, he was racing down the front path after Percy. "You'll have to drive," gasped Stan, still clutching his broken hand. "And get me to a hospital quick. That old shit bag's a total sodding lunatic."

Still euphoric over finally getting hold of the package, Percy was in a mood to be generous and told Stan that he would certainly drop him off at a hospital, but couldn't hang around to help him any further as he had a most important appointment in London. He was sure that Stan would get all the help he needed in getting back to London whenever. Sitting back comfortably in his seat, he let slip the clutch in order to roar up Northbrooke Road. Or rather, he thought he was going to roar up the avenue. Instead, he skidded, swerved, bumped and spun across the intersection with Cranbrooke Avenue, his bonnet smashing straight into the front of the spare Traffic Warden cone van that had just rounded the corner.

"It's the tyres". Shouted Percy. "The bloody, sodding tyres are flat. I couldn't steer."

He savagely rammed the car into reverse and ramped up the revs, but while the wheels started to spin at ever increasing speed causing billowing clouds of blue smoke to spread across the street, the car could not pull itself out of its entanglement with the cone van.

Percy turned savagely towards Stan. "Stop bloody moaning and whining like a little kid you great pussy and get out there and see if you can get the car free. Go on! Get out! Now you bastard."

A red faced, furiously angry Polly arrived at the window of Percy's car just as Stan launched himself at his boss. Broken hand notwithstanding, Stan's blood was up. His hand hurt no more and with broken fingers and torn tendons, it joined with his uninjured hand in trying to strangle Percy as he rammed his face into the steering wheel.

"Take that you shit," he shouted as he heard Percy's nose break. "And that, and that". He broke off, gasping with the pain of his ruined hand.

"Tango Whisky 08 to control. Require police assistance at Northbrooke Road intersection with Cranbrook. Two males fighting, repeat two males fighting. Over. Oh and get an ambulance as well you might as well. There's blood and stuff all over."

She thrust her head into the car window inches from Percy's reddening, blood covered face.

"You bastard! You've written off the bloody cone van. My cone van. What the fuck did you think you were doing? And stop that bloody fighting, the pair of you."

"My Bill would never have crashed into a cone van………"

"Oh for God's sake Henrietta. I don't give a stuff what your Bill would have done, now just get round to the………" The rest of her sentence was lost as the radio blared.

"Tango Whisky 008. Tango Whisky 08. Come in Polly. Have you located Reggie yet? Is that a police siren Polly? Update please. Over." Polly wrenched the radio off her belt and spat into it.

"Oh piss off will you Barbara. We're a bit busy here right now. Out."

Reggie and Phyllis looked on then developing scene with a growing sense of unease. It was evident that things were getting serious and that bad people were involved in something and that something was all to do with the package that Reggie had pocketed after the robbery attempt that he had supposedly foiled. All this had managed to penetrate Reggie's mind at last and he was becoming ever more grateful that Phyllis had taken a hand in all this. He knew his limitations and one of these was that his bravado was a theoretical notion, not something to be tested in practice and it was getting dangerously close to that point where he might just have to actually do something brave. He also had a gut feeling that Phyllis, this new woman in his life, knew all this and somehow accepted it and would protect him from harm.

"Sounded more like a pussy than a tough guy, all that screaming an' all." said Phyllis. "I hope your mum's OK."

"She'll be OK, don't you worry mumbled Reggie but I'm a bit worried about what she gave him. I hope it wasn't that package. Phyllis, drive round the back and I'll nip in and see what happened."

"You reckon she could have given him the package?" asked Phyllis. "That'd be no good at all after all this."

"No, not that." Answered Reggie almost looking embarrassed. "Ah, here we are. Look, wait here. I'll just nip in and see what Mum's been up to." He leaped out of the car, opened the small back gate and rushed up the path to his house. Phyllis, worried that Reggie might yet mess up a little followed him.

"Your mates came round Reggie. I thought they were those vacuum cleaner bag people so I gave 'em the package, don't you worry. I told 'em we knew all about vacuum cleaner bags, but he wouldn't listen. Just kept screaming about something. Rude sod! 'ow many packages have you got then? I found another one in those warden trousers of yours. In the pocket. Interesting. It's a flash drive. Two Gigs. That's a lot of info these days Reggie, but it wasn't very interesting. I got through the password, no probs. Someone's accounts I think. Pictures of rockets as well, and that government bloke…what's his name. Gormless looking sod. Got no chin. Put tickets on rockets now do you? Times are really changing. Cars I thought, but rockets as well? I told 'em we'd got all the vacuum cleaner bags we needed and we didn't want no rockets neither, but he kept screaming like a kid, silly sod, and then his mate grabbed the package and hightailed it off down………."

Reggie knew that he'd have to cut in. His dear old mum could go on like this until she fell asleep if he let her. Whether worrying obsessively about vacuum cleaner bags or trying to hack into GCHQs secrets, his mum could, at the same time, talk and moan for England. Most it utter nonsense but in there somewhere were gems.

"It's OK mum. You did just right. It's true, we don't need any cleaner bags." Reggie's mum brightened at this welcoming news and the assurance that she'd done right.

"But mum, where's the package from my trousers. You know, the one with the flash drive?"

"In the computer Reggie. Where else would it be. That's where flash drives live. That's what they're for. Look, this is how they fit. I told 'em well and good that we didn't want no cleaner bags. Told 'em to piss off. They're no good for computers are they Reggie. No rockets in them, that's the problem with vacuum cleaner bags. Don't even need a password, don't cleaner bags. Stupid things. It's that one over there. I won't put it in my notebook cos of bugs. Before you take it Reggie, I'd better copy it. I'll do it now. Then I can hide it in all sorts of places. Their passwords are easy. Screaming his head off he was. There! Oh no, it won't copy. Blocked from that it is. I could've spread it about now Reggie, but no good. Is that all right? I need a lie down now Reggie. G'night Reggie. You looked so sweet, all tucked up in your pyjamas. Muffin the mule ones I got for you didn't I?.......I'll bet you.........oh! I'm so tired now Reggie....." Mrs Parkes sank gently down onto the sofa as verbal exhaustion overtook her and from where low snores immediately began to emanate.

'At last' thought Reggie as he shot across to the main computer. He wasn't sure just what his mum had done but he knew that for at least half an hour he'd have a bit of peace. His mum would sleep like a baby for now. He grabbed the drive from its socket, put a blanket over his mum and slipped out the back to the waiting, widely grinning Phyllis.

"Muffin the mule? Muffin the bloody mule! Did you really wear Muffin the mule pyjamas Reggie? I knew there was something odd about you Reggie Parkes." Phyllis collapsed laughing in her seat.

"Yeah well." Muttered Reggie, turning scarlet as he tried to think of a suitably cutting reply and wishing that Phyllis hadn't heard that. "But at least we've got what was in the package."

"That's true and after we've had a good look at it we can decide just how much trouble you're in Reggie Parkes and then we can decide what we're going to do about it. Eh Muffin?"

Reggie scowled, but then sat back contentedly. Despite the piss taking over the Muffin the mule pyjamas, it was good to have someone make decisions for him, especially at the moment when everything seemed to have turned upside down in his life. He'd spent so long sorting his old mum out, or trying to at least, that to have someone else make decisions seemed like paradise. Ever since he was 16 when his dad died, he'd had to care for his mum. There had been no time for study at uni or have girlfriends. He'd just had to work to get some money and take responsibility for his batty old mum. And God knows, that wasn't easy at times. He knew it had turned him a bit odd in turn and he knew in himself that all his boasting about his mythical achievements in life were just a cover for having to lead the dullest life on earth. But his Walter Mitty like stories and boasts were an escape from his personal prison even though they drew shit loads of piss taking from the others. Despite all this, he had accepted his lot and was more or less content with life, but now with Phyllis beginning to call the shots in his life, things were definitely looking up. But suddenly remembering what he was meant to be thinking about, he realised that he had forgotten to ask what exactly was in the package that his mum had given to Percy. He knew it wasn't the flash drive but he had a nagging feeling that it was his new teeth that had arrived yesterday, and he really could have done with them.

"Come on Reggie. We've got to get out of here. I can hear sirens. We don't want the police finding you yet do we?" Phyllis slipped her little car into gear and they headed off back to Shelley Mansions, both pleased with the way matters were turning out.

Chapter Eleven

"So let's get this straight Barbara shall we?" Chief Superintendent Montagu Matthews looked down at his paper wearily and started his recital. "Reggie Parkes, our Traffic Warden hero of the recent gun incident has gone missing, supposedly with an item belonging to the British Home Office in his possession, which he stole from an officer of that same office, after badly injuring another employee of that office, and for which item he later substituted a set of dentures passed to the said employee by his slightly demented, and from what I understand, extremely aggressive mother. In connection with all this, whilst under your orders to look for Parkes, one of your Traffic Wardens drove a police owned cone van into - and I mean actually right into the Pig and Whistle public house, causing what has been estimated at £179,000 worth of damage, and giving the bar maid a fit of the vapours, as well as writing off the van of course. Also in connection with this Parkes business, another of your Traffic Wardens crashed another police owned cone van - your second and last I might add, into the car of the very same officer of the Home Office, writing off both vehicles and further exacerbating the injuries of the other aforesaid employee of the Home Office who is now in hospital with 4 broken fingers, glass abrasion to his face, three torn tendons and a dislocated shoulder, with the other employee suffering a broken nose and strangely enough, symptoms of strangulation. And despite the importance of this Parkes investigation to the government and therefore to the police, the main investigating officer is reportedly at a funeral in Weymouth, having for some reason - and I find this hard to believe Barbara, decided to attend on the spur of the moment, in place of Sergeant Fisher who had come in off leave specially to go to Weymouth, and that now, DI Brightwell is unable to return from the funeral until he has given the customary funeral oration on behalf of the police and had a nice chat with the widow over tea and cakes. Have I left anything out Barbara or could there be even more to add to this sorry affair?"

"I didn't know about Dibsey and the funeral sir, but for the rest, I think that about sums it up," said Barbara warily. She knew Monty of old and knew that after a long and so far distinguished career, his promotion to a Chief Constable role with a knighthood, was his main and overarching priority at the moment and if not that, a comfortable and honourable retirement to the country. Now this Reggie business was beginning to get a bit out of control. In fact, completely out of control if she really thought about it.

"But you might want to add sir that we still haven't managed to locate Traffic Warden Parkes. Yet! We are still looking, but of course we are now completely on foot. The two vans are……..."

"Yes, I know just how the vans are Barbara, thank you. They have both been written off actually. As has the Home Office vehicle. I say this in case you were under any illusion as to the current road worthiness of any of these vehicles."

Monty wiped his brow. He wore a pained look on his face as he looked across the table at this usually very able woman. Monty had risen in the ranks from office tea boy at 14, to police constable at 17 and had since those far off days passed through the ranks to Chief Superintendent the hard way. No favouritism for him, no 'connections' in the force; no top school background and not even a friend in government, he thought grimly. Working class dad, five good O-levels from grammar school and at each step of the way he had had to fight for promotion and beat off the competition, which admittedly, he had done with professionalism. He was simply a good cop and he'd seen them all off. All his rivals had fallen by the wayside, and now the top job was within his grasp - and of course the possibility of an attendant knighthood. Sir Montagu Matthews, knight of the realm; Chief Constable of the county police force, and Lady Doris Matthews his dear wife. If only he could get that prize for Doris. Her Ladyship! He sat back, his eyes glazed and a light smile lit his face. Sir Montagu and Lady…….

"Are you alright sir?" said Barbara in alarm. "You're not having a turn are you sir?"

Monty jerked his head round to look at her, his mind snapping back immediately to the business in hand.

"Barbara, I don't have turns if you don't mind. I was simply trying to sort out in my mind a logical sequence of required actions to conclude once and for all this Traffic Warden Parkes business. It's evident that you've got to find him first and find out why he's disappeared and what he's up to and more importantly, what he's alleged to be holding. I've spoken to Councillor Dillon, your admin boss at the Council and he's agreed that until the end of the party conference, the Traffic Wardens or whatever you're called now, revert to Police control. It's quite sensible because otherwise we'll all be pulling in different directions and as we're all paranoid over terrorist actions these days, and what with this Parkes business, I'm content with that. Anything to say?"

Barbara shook her head.

"So gather your troops in; brief them fully on the situation to date and send them out again to find the wretched man. Concentrate on his house or the houses of any of his known associates. He's hardly going to live rough is he? I can't spare a single constable for this at the moment. They're totally tied up with the party conference in town, but in an emergency, I can bring in some wardens from some of the other boroughs, and you can always call the duty Sergeant if really mega urgent help is needed. Oh, and you can take one more van out of the pool, but for

God's sake put someone in charge of it that knows how to drive and that excludes all the other clowns that have caused so much damage today. Keep me up to date Barbara. I want a call on the hour. Every hour. Got it?"

"Yes sir," said Barbara, itching to get out of his office and get to work. She really needed something positive to do even if only to keep her mind off her herpes and piles.

Monty looked at her keenly. He knew that many people thought him a bit of a pain in the arse; a buffoon indeed, but they simply didn't realise the horrors of the political and politically correct environment that he worked in. He had survived as a Chief Superintendent only by learning to swim in that environment and by avoiding the many sharks and shoals of piranha fish that lurked in the darker corners, and of course by being smarter than the average rival - especially when it came to realising his goal of attaining a knighthood. And probably because of his smarter than average outlook, he was disturbed by this Parkes business. Something smelled bad here, and he wanted to know what it was.

He softened his voice and looked over at Barbara. "Before you go Barbara. There's something strange about this whole business, isn't there?" He carried on without waiting for an answer. "Reggie Parkes. I've read his annual performance reports and he's not the disappearing sort is he?"

"Not at all sir," replied Barbara.

"And he's not the hero sort either, is he?"

"Far from it," said Barbara.

"And senior policemen don't 'accidentally' end up at funerals and miss out on interviews, when Foreign Office officials come to town, even Dibsey, do they?"

"Not usually at all," replied Barbara wondering where all this was leading.

"And Barbara, the second van crashed looking for Reggie. It crashed into the Home Office car near Reggie's mum's house. so it appears they were looking for Reggie as well. And they didn't ask us - or you. And we are the police. And the HO is sending some more people down to 'help' us in our enquiries. It's odd isn't it? They're just not satisfied with a set of dentures evidently!"

Barbara finally saw where he was going.

"Barbara. My hunch is that Reggie thinks he is in some sort of trouble as a result of that robbery business and even I think that everything here isn't what it seems. Go find him. I'll try and provide any cover here if you need it, and I'll have a discreet look into these HO johnnies. Just get it sorted OK? Oh, and don't talk about this terrorism bit to anyone will you. I'm not sure what it's all about and in fact I think it's just something dreamed up by these London people but we don't want to frighten anyone, do we?"

"I'll get it sorted sir, don't you worry." Barbara, anxious to get to work and immensely relieved that someone in authority would provide some cover, even though she knew this was limited to what would advance his aim of getting that knighthood stood up carefully and strode from his office.

Monty sat back in his chair. 'Lady Matthews', he thought. A very nice ring to it. Doris would like that. But first Reggie Parkes. His brow clouded over. He picked up the phone.

Chapter Twelve

Dibsey was red faced, furious, worried, anxious and outraged all at the same time as he strode hurriedly back to the patiently waiting driver and the official car. His phone had eight missed calls on it, four of them from the Chief Super, three from that bloody Traffic Warden woman and one from police central and he knew he was in some sort of shit. He had managed to get a quick text off to the Chief Super briefly explaining his plight, but then the Vicar had interrupted that by asking him to come up and provide the congregation with his oration. That bloody Percy bloke from London and his yobbo driver were going to get a piece of his mind when he got back to the office and no mistake. He'd get his bloody revenge on those bastards. His mind whirled around that central thought. The 'quick' funeral service promised by the vicar had droned on for an hour and a half and he'd had to be woken up when he had slumped down in his pew, and after that, half the bloody county had stepped up to say a 'few words' which had covered another 45 minutes of sickening, sycophantic crap. Then he'd been asked to give the police oration over which he had stumbled and strained and had even at one critical point forgotten the deceased sergeant's name in all the confusion. His short, but required chat to the widowed Myrtle Boniface over a cup of tea had wasted another hour during which he had tried desperately to get away on numerous occasions only to be thwarted in his endeavours by her, sudden, unbelievably strong and very bony grip! He thought back to how each time he had smilingly tried to rise, she had gripped his arm in a vice like hold and pulled him down again. But finally she had relented because she needed to go to the toilet, and this gave him his opportunity to slip away quickly as soon as she'd left the room. His relief knew no bounds when at last he was away from it all and was striding out of the sitting room, even as the vicar and a young journalist girl who had been tasked to write a report about the funeral for the local rag loomed up on his left.

"Oh, thank you Inspector for such a fine oration," began the Vicar. "Mrs Boniface was so thrilled to see……."

"Vicar," shouted Dibsey, desperately and shrilly. He collected himself and lowered his voice. "Vicar, I'm so sorry, but I've just had a most urgent call to get back as soon as possible. A terrorist incident….. " Dibsey thought frantically for something that would give the vicar the idea that he really had to leave immediately and he didn't think that the word 'terrorist' was stretching it too far. The Reggie Parkes business had been referred to as having terrorism overtones after all and Parkes was wanted for a terrorist offence - not that Dibsey could think what possible reason anyone had for saying that. But they had. He kept up his fast pace to the waiting car

"It's most urgent I'm afraid Vicar," he lied desperately. "Terrorism. Defence of the homeland and all that. Remember, there is a party conference going on in town. These big political events always attract all the crazies. The PM's there you know. People might be injured. Dead most probably. Might even be a conference lock down." He was babbling now. "Got to go. Good bye Vicar." He was sweating freely as he reached the car, not really caring what he said, or what they believed as long as he could get away, his face a mask of desperation to escape.

He stepped into the car, the door held open by the still very patient driver and sank down gratefully into the soft, leather seat. The girl took a photograph. The door shut, the driver got behind the wheel, and finally, with a totally mentally exhausted Detective Inspector flopped down in the back seat, and the car drew away and headed back to where Dibsey knew he ought to be. There would be a pile of very deep shit to face when he got back, but at that moment, he didn't care. He had escaped.

Barbara surveyed her troops across the briefing room, their numbers augmented by those who had called in as supposedly sick that morning, but now remarkably felt themselves better even before their three day period without having to produce a certificate was up. The word had evidently got around to even these that something momentous was going on and no-one wanted to miss any of the fun. The loud hum of expectant conversation filled the room and questions and answers flew back and forth between those who generally didn't know what they were talking about but felt the need to comment anyway. Dave, Keith and Dan stood nervously at the back of the crowd, not wanting to expose themselves to any form of ridicule from their assembled colleagues and they were flanked by the equally nervous Polly and Henrietta who were also worried about their future as Traffic Wardens in view of the business with the Foreign Office car.

"Quiet everyone please," shouted Barbara over the hubbub of voices, and was gratified when silence returned to the room.

"Thank you all for coming in so promptly. Now you all know about the Reggie Parkes hero business that happened a few weeks ago and that he's now back to work. You'll also probably know that we've been looking for Reggie today and whilst doing so we had a couple of accidents with the vans and a couple of injuries. Although no injuries to any of us Traffic Wardens, thank goodness."

The room giggled and looked round at the red faced group at the back.

"Desperate for a pint was yer?" a voice from near the front. "Bloody good parking there Dan. Right up to the bar. Bloody brilliant man. Even funnier than Keith and his arse cones." The room erupted in laughter. Dan and Keith looked at him murderously.

"Told yer women shouldn't be driving them vans. Gawd 'elp us. They'll get the bloody vote next! You just wait and see!" Another voice to the left of the room. Henrietta held Polly back as a female chorus of 'piss offs' and 'male chauvinist pricks' and other generally unsavoury phrases were hurled across the room at the speaker.

"OK, OK," roared Barbara. "That's enough. This is a serious business and I want all of your attention. Now!" The room subsided.

"Now pay attention and have your fun later. The simple facts are that we need to speak to Reggie and we don't know where he is. It seems that others also want to speak to Reggie and we are not exactly sure why, and we think he may be keeping low so as to avoid them. The Chief Super has asked that we get to him first. He reckons that Reggie might think he's in trouble of some kind and indeed he may well be. But it's gone far enough that we think he may be in a bit of danger. He may need our help and I hope you are up to it. Remember, he's one of us."

The Traffic Wardens, open mouthed and casting amazed glances at each other, nodded in agreement. That was right. He was one of us. A complete pain in the arse most of the time of course, but as the lady said, one of us, so naturally we'll help. This was indeed serious stuff concerning someone they could call a brother in arms and they were all eager to get involved.

"Now as I said, we would prefer that we found Reggie before anyone else. That's point number one. Is that clear?" The troops nodded.

"Now it's getting late today so I'll hand each of you an assigned area based on Reggie's past history and you look and you ask and you talk to people. You'll be in pairs and you keep your radios on and no canteen. The Police are 'lending' us a van on the strict understanding that it is returned in one piece in a spotless condition. Jan, you'll take the van as you're the only person I trust not to crash the bloody thing. It's one of the new models and you'll take Dave along with you and you'll keep an eye on Reggie's street area. Any suspicious cars or people, I want to know. And if you crash it, you're dead. OK?"

Dan listened to Barbara with increasing gloom. He should have the van, not some fliberty gibbert like Jan. It was unfair of Barbara, and he was mightily pissed off about the whole thing. It was his van by rights. That Pig business could have happened to anyone. It was wrong of her and it made him feel disloyal.

Jan on the other hand, delighted to get the van driver position off Dan, nodded enthusiastically to Barbara and beckoned to Dave to come over to her. She liked Dave; she didn't know him well but he seemed one of the more sensible and educated wardens. No face about him, and he was a looker. There were possibilities with Dave, she thought. She glanced over at him and found him glancing back. She smiled and looked away.

Barbara continued. "At cease work everyone, report back here and if necessary we'll start again in the morning after the usual briefing. Now get moving and start talking and listen out on your radios. If I call, I want answers immediately and if anyone tells me to fuck off over the radio again, they're also dead. Got it?"

I'll need extra chairs tomorrow she thought. I've never seen so many of them together except at the Christmas do which was free.

The room moved to the table to collect the slips with their assigned patrol areas and two by two they gradually exited the room. Barbara, glad to have got all that out of the way and happy in the knowledge that she had done everything possible to direct the effort, shuffled off to the loo for an urgent application of calendula cream. She still had that nagging feeling though at the back of her mind, that something was not quite right with any of this. Why was Reggie in trouble? Where was he? Why were people from London involved? Why had Dibsey gone to a funeral in Weymouth when he knew that all the action was here? It seemed to be getting more and more difficult to put her finger on anything, let alone one solid fact or answer. It was like trying to grab hold of a cloud, and the effects on her herpes and piles were a painful and very itchy manifestation of all this worry.

Jan and Dave went round to the police vehicle pound and clambered into a brand new, top of the range police van with those fast, multi-coloured flashing lights and a whole variety of sound effects available at the push of a button. Jan's eyes lit up in delight, and not only because she was driving a new van with automatic transmission and proper bells and whistles. She looked round coyly at Dave as she eased it out of the compound and then immediately faced the front as she started to fret about the huge zit on her face that she had exploded only that very morning while arguing on the phone with Henrietta over the firm banana business.

Dibsey bounded up the steps to the police station anxious to give some sort of explanation of his absence to his Chief Super. He had had plenty of time to think of every excuse under the sun, having already received a bollocking of the first order from the Chief Super by phone during the long car ride home, but in the end he had decided just to front up and admit having made a cock up in his eagerness to sort out the Parkes business. What with road works, a funeral procession and a flooded main blocking the Dorchester road, it had taken him nearly two hours to get back to the police station and he knew that the Chief wanted to get home on time that day to celebrate

Doris's birthday so he wasn't expecting a great welcome exactly, but what he got easily exceeded all his already low expectations.

"What the fucking hell have you been up to you incompetent prick?" snarled Monty as soon as Dibsey entered his office. He waived a copy of the evening edition of the Westbourne Globe in Dibsey's face and hurled it at him. Dibsey read with growing horror the huge headlines splashed across the front page. "What the bloody hell is all this about Officer fucking Dribble?"

"TERRORISTS SHUT DOWN WESTBOURNE PARTY CONFERENCE. PRIME MINISTER CAUGHT IN CENTRE LOCK DOWN."

And there almost as large as life below the accusing words was a full colour picture of a worried looking Dibsey himself getting into the police car at Sergeant Boniface's funeral with the caption;

"TOP COP WARNS OF TERRORIST ACTION. HEADS URGENTLY TO THE SCENE. MANY THOUGHT DEAD." EXCLUSIVE

"Our Gazette reporter on the spot, Jennifer Johnson writes that just two hours ago, Detective Inspector Barney Brightwell, one of the county's top police officers warned of on-going terrorist action directed against the party conference in Westbourne

today. He reported that there may be many deaths so far with action expected…………………"

He stopped reading and looked up in horror at his boss.

"Well? And it had better be good Brightwell because the local Council and every other bloody organisation in town is demanding that the situation be sorted as people are getting really worried, and so the bloody army has been put on standby by the Home Secretary and his defence counterpart. The Chief Constable has ordered the conference centre to be placed under lock down 'just in case' you were right and is in the mood for murder. And as for you, you've got a fucking hell of a lot of explaining to do and however well you explain it, you're still in the deepest shit ever known to man. Got that? And I never said you could sit down. Get up."

The phone rang. "Yes ma'm. Yes ma'm. Right away ma'm. On my way ma'm. I'll bring him ma'm. And the Head Traffic Warden? Yes, they are under Police control for the duration of the conference. Yes, fully agreed to by the Council. Right away ma'm." Monty stood up and looked over at Dibsey, his face a mask. "That was the Chief Constable. She wants to see us both, and your friend Barbara. Now!"

Jennifer Johnson, new cub reporter to Southern Globe Press that included the Westbourne Gazette knew she had done well with her very first syndicated, published report, when her editor who previously had only ever spoken to her once when she first started, called her into his office to personally congratulate her on the best scoop for the paper since VE Day. Her report had been syndicated all over the UK, Europe and the USA and various other places, and he had even passed nice comments about her photography. She had caught the urgency and worry expressed by Detective Inspector Brightwell just perfectly and her report had put the Globe well and truly in the national and international spotlight. Her dad had always told her that it's amazing just what you can pick up at a good funeral, and he was right. Good old dad she thought. He'd be proud of her when he saw the papers. She decided not to say anything so that it would be a nice surprise for him. True, other, more experienced reporters had been sent to Westbourne to cover the unfolding story, but it had been her by-line on the actual scoop. *An exclusive report from our Gazette reporter on the spot, Jennifer Johnson'*. She walked home a happy girl that evening, with thoughts of the Times of London, foreign postings and the adventures of war correspondents drifting around gently and fuzzily in her happy head.

Chapter Thirteen

Reggie was getting a bit worried about things. It was all very well imagining being a super hero and facing off gun toting criminals, but actually having to live up to such an imagined reputation was another matter altogether. Despatched to the corner shop by Phyllis to buy something for tea, he'd seen the headlines splashed all over the billboards outside the shop. 'Terrorists' he thought worriedly. 'They said I'm a terrorist and now they're sending in the army to get me.' Grabbing a pack of his favourites; chicken nuggets and some frozen chips, he quickly paid and left the shop, then shot back for a bottle of tomato sauce, an essential accompaniment. No need to worry about booze he thought. Phyllis always seems to have an ample stock in the larder. Another good point about the woman. She'd already started planning what to do about the package and even if that failed, solace could always be found in her ample larder where the whisky was to be found.

"Seems to me that it's all about that package Reggie. Now the easiest thing would be to just hand it into Dibsey and forget all about it. Return to normal."

Reggie looked alarmed. Normal, he thought? He wasn't at all sure he wanted to return to Normal. Normal meant slagging off Mrs Elworthy and having the Traffic Wardens always taking the piss; and being sole carer for his mum; and that wasn't easy. In this new, improved environment, old bat Elworthy had become Phyllis, and the Traffic Wardens were a bit more respectful due to his hero act which even they couldn't gainsay. No, he thought. Don't want no going back to normal. Even mum seemed to be more lively now after seeing the flash drive in the package. And that got him to thinking. Mum said there were diagrams of rockets on the stick and to Reggie; that meant only one thing. In fact, when he thought a bit more it meant several things. All of them trouble. Arms; spying; money; danger; bullets and guns, and he already knew about that last bit. He'd got a wound to prove it. Returning to normal now would be unthinkable. Then he brightened as Phyllis carried on.

"But we don't know about Dibsey yet do we? I mean he's on the same side as those goons from London who threatened you. And that flash drive seems to have some bloody dangerous stuff on it from what your mum says. I mean, rockets and stuff. That's arms isn't it? You read stuff about that all the time in the paper. Let's have a look at it on my computer and see."

They went into the dining room where Phyllis kept her large, old computer and they sat staring at it in silence as it wound itself up. Finally, as Phyllis's screen page assembled itself into a picture of a giant bottle of Grant's Whisky, she put the flash drive into the slot and opened it.

"There are four files here Reggie." She looked round at him to make sure he was paying attention, and then clicked on the first one to open it. 'Enter Password' immediately appeared in front of them. After trying all four files, she again looked round at Reggie. "We're going to have to fetch your mum along Reggie and that's probably good anyway. What with those goons going round to your house, you never know how your mum will cope if they pay another visit. They're not going to be fobbed off with another set of teeth are they?"

Reggie looked at her in alarm. He hadn't thought of that. Here was another example of Phyllis's clear thinking. He had to act immediately. Mum shouldn't be left in any danger. Why hadn't he thought of that?

"I'll go round and get her now. I've got to check on Star and Mercury anyway. See they're fed and so on. Roxy might be able to come down for a while to look after things. I haven't heard from her for ages but I'll give her a ring. She's up in London doing her thing whatever that is. Modelling and such like." Reggie was never sure what exactly Roxy did for a living, but she seemed to live very well anyway, bless her. He rose from his chair by the computer and hurriedly started to put his jacket on.

"No Reggie," said Phyllis. We can go and get her in my car. It'd be quicker and safer. I'll just hide the stick and we can get going. When we get there, tell your mum to quickly pack a few things for a few nights, but tell her to do it quick. We don't want to be there if there's another visit by hostiles."

Reggie looked at her in amazement. She even knew the right terms to use, just like in the movies. Hostiles! It summed those bastards up perfectly. She was awesome.

"C'mon Reggie, let's go get mum."

Lennie Pratt was happy to be going down to the seaside, especially as it was on government business and so it was all expenses paid. You didn't get many of them nowadays. But since the sad demise of Percy and Stan who had somehow screwed up a very simple operation, and seemingly set the town on a major non-existent terrorist alert, Lennie had been chosen by the Gods on high to follow up and clean up. And this he was determined to do, under the general direction of Salim Malek his hardnosed, inscrutable, Anglo Arab, Coptic Christian, naturalised British boss who sat by himself on the back seat of the car. There would be no cock-ups with this guy in charge thought Lennie. Especially if all they had to deal with was a Traffic Warden and his simple minded old mum. He looked forward to it, and as instructed, headed directly to 39 Northbrooke Road, where this so called Traffic Warden hero lived. Salim wanted a recce; to see the lie of the land before heading for the police headquarters to call in on a certain Detective

Inspector Brightwell. Whatever else happened, he'd get that package back. The Home Secretary himself wanted it for the Prime Minister and had left Salim in no doubt about what would happen to him if he failed.

"ETA Northbrooke Road, ten minutes boss," he called over to the back. He was rewarded with a brief nod and a grunt. No, thought Lennie. There would be no mess-ups with this guy.

Chapter Fourteen

Jan was definitely wearing her happy head as she sped along Larch Road. The new van was great; fast, comfortable and equipped with every device known to man - or woman, to make driving it a pleasure. And not only that, she had the lovely Dave Keenan sitting beside her, looking steely and hero like. Absolute happiness would have been possible had the major zit business not been troubling her. But as long as she looked straight ahead, she thought Dave wouldn't notice it. She knew her profile looked pretty good anyway.

"OK Jan, I reckon our first port of call is Reggie's house in Northbrooke Road. You never know, he might be there, and I know his mum lives there and she might know his whereabouts. Mind you, from what I remember she's as batty as hell."

"Northbrooke it is Dave," as she turned into Langley Crescent. She had almost simpered then she thought. Must stop that and try and sound normal and a bit more business-like. She lowered her voice. "Be there in about ten."

Phyllis parked in the back lane behind the row of houses and waited patiently in the car for Reggie to sort things out and get his mum. Treading slowly and carefully, in case of watchers - Phyllis had rightly warned him about these, Reggie quietly unlocked the back gate and swiftly going up to the house, banged on the back door of his house and looked in the kitchen window. His mum was just putting the kettle on the gas stove and looked up in alarm at Reggie before smiling in relief. As Reggie entered the kitchen she immediately started babbling about rockets and asked Reggie if he wanted tea.

Reggie cut in hurriedly, knowing that if he let her rabbit on, his quick visit could take hours. "Mum, we need your help with a computer in Phyllis's house. Now get a few things, clothes and the like for a few days and we'll go right now."

"Is that your young lady Reggie? The one that likes rockets?"

"Rockets? Oh yeah, yeah of course. Yeah, that's the one mum, now come on love, let's get moving quick like."

He sprinted upstairs and grabbed some of her wardrobe, undies and bras from the drawer and some cosmetics from the bathroom, thinking he could return for whatever else she needed later, and stuffed them into a suitcase and ran downstairs. He also grabbed her laptop and charger from the sitting room and grabbing her elbow, eased her out of the kitchen, down the path and into the waiting car. You had to be like that with mum, or even the simplest thing could take all day to accomplish.

"Hi Mrs Parkes," said Phyllis from the front. "You look nice today dear. We need your help you know."

"So I heard." Sniffed Reggie's mum clearly annoyed about missing her tea. "I hope I haven't left the gas on you know. Cos I never lit it. There's no clicker anymore. It broke years ago and you need matches. Everything was such a rush. It was like that with the vacuum cleaner bag people. All rush and hurry and then the rockets! I mean, what can you do? Reggie, what can you do?"

"It's OK mum," said Reggie. Phyllis has got a good house and you'll like the bedroom." He stopped suddenly and looked furtively at Phyllis. He hadn't thought about bedrooms and things of that nature. Phyllis only had two bedrooms. One with a double bed and the other with a single. So what was he to do? What was Phyllis thinking? It was all very well getting to know a woman, as he had done with Phyllis, but how did one progress from there. He had to admit to himself that he had absolutely no experience of this sort of thing. Sure, he knew the theory and had read all the books and looked furtively at a few magazines graphically depicting the subject, but it was becoming very evident now that he had no idea about the actual practice of the matter. He looked again at Phyllis. She looked back and raised her eyebrow at him and smiled. He looked ahead and gulped. She roared off as fast as her Lada could manage, imagining all sorts of things that she thought she had forgotten all about following the demise of old Mr Elworthy, and with her thoughts racing, she realised that she had just shot a red light, or very nearly so; something she had never done in her life before. Rapidly sobering her thoughts and slowing down to the usual Phyllis crawl, she headed steadily back to Shelley mansions.

"Here we are," said Phyllis. "All safe and sound and now we can all have a nice cup of tea before looking at the computer and sorting the beds out."

Reggie faced the front and said nothing.

Reggie's mum had fallen fast asleep in the back and was snoring loudly.

The elderly looking man in the small green van parked just across the road, watched them walk into the lobby of Shelley mansions, and being a very thorough man, decided to make sure they were who he thought they were before relaying the information to his boss.

Chapter Fifteen

"There you go boss," said Lennie with satisfaction at having navigated a most direct route to Northbrooke Road. "Number 39. All yours." He parked up at the kerb on the opposite side of the road and they both looked over at number 39.

"It looks empty boss, but you never know. Apparently his mum is a bit batty. Shall I go and have a closer look?"

"Yes. But first drive round the corner and park there. Out of sight, out of mind as we British say. There may be other eyes around the place. After we have parked, we can wander around to the house." The very precise and clipped tones of his boss came from the back of the car. "You can pretend to deliver a parcel and make a point of looking for a suitable place to put it if there is no reply to your knock." A well wrapped parcel appeared from the back. Salim thought of everything. "In the meantime, I will wander up the street and casually look around."

Grasping the parcel, Lennie slid out of the car and headed over to the house. There didn't appear to be any interest whatsoever in their presence from other houses and he knocked loudly on the door. There was no answer and like most people legitimately looking for a house occupant, he took a peek through the letter box to see if anyone was around. There was no-one but there was a bit of an off smell coming from the house. Gassy, he thought. Must be the septic. 'Ah well,' thought Lennie, 'I'll go round the back and see if there's anyone there. Got to act like a normal person who isn't hiding anything. Perhaps I'll have a quick fag round the back as well. Been dying for one ever since London.' The back garden was empty as well and Lennie couldn't see anyone in the house. Perhaps now would be a good time for a little break in, he thought, but dismissed the idea immediately. Must get that sort of decision from Salim, otherwise there would be no end of trouble. He got out his cigarettes and moved behind the old concrete coal bunker.

As he walked slowly up the road, politely saying hello to a couple walking their dog, Salim looked around at the area. He was interested in all things British, both the best and the worst, and here, he thought, we have some of the worst. Typical British lower class, he thought. Small, mean semi-detached houses in a small mean street, made even worse by the huge electricity station just up the road. He was glad he had come to Britain and was pleased to call himself British and in fact was very pro-British, but some of their housing left so much to be desired, as did their weather. Mind you, he thought again, these little houses would be veritable palaces compared to some of the dwellings in Alexandria, his original home. He turned again to retrace his steps back to the car, thinking about his presence there. This was an awkward little mission and below him, he felt, but after all he had been sent in after someone else had screwed up and so perhaps it was going to be more challenging than it seemed at first. Yes, he thought, as he watched a police van come round the corner and slowly make its way up the road. We'd better leave now and make our way to the police HQ. We don't want to make problems until we have to.

It never ceased to surprise Dame Elizabeth Longstaff, Chief Constable of the County, just how quickly and unexpectedly, tiny little things could suddenly and incredibly rapidly, grow into big things, then giant things and then get so big that they explode in your face like an atom bomb, covering everyone for miles around in crap. Rank was irrelevant to the process; in fact, the higher up in the hierarchy you were, the deeper the shit that you found yourself in after said explosion had occurred. It had happened throughout her career and it was only her innate ability to dodge fast moving bullets and the inevitable shit sprays that came her way quicker than her colleagues, that had enabled her advancement to her present comfortable rank faster than anyone else. Known to all in the force as Slippery Liz, she took on board immediately that this Traffic Warden business was just such an incident, but she was totally confident in her ability to deal quickly with the matter, and also to enhance her own image in the process. The addition of overtones of terrorism were an added bonus for her; after all, all it really boiled down to was the mad antics of a few seemingly retarded Traffic Wardens, getting involved in robberies gone wrong and smashing down pubs. Sort them out and she would have calmed a terrorist scenario, to her credit. She wondered at times why she was getting involved at all, but when you had the Prime Minister and most of his party locked in a conference hall in the county town, even she realised that her active involvement was required and she was pondering the minor issues involved when her three subordinates arrived for their meeting.

Civility was one of Liz's trademarks and she greeted them all very cordially, inviting them to take tea and an Anzac biscuit, imported especially from New Zealand, in a handsome tin, depicting sailors returning from the war and being greeted by their waiting families. "Now lady and gentlemen," she began. "Matters seem to be getting a tadge out of hand with this Traffic Warden business, don't they?" She looked curiously at Barbara. They had never previously met, but Liz could see in this head of Traffic Wardens someone of perhaps equal steel to her own. Or nearly at any rate; but she did seem to be sitting in a slightly awkward manner. Quite odd, she thought.

"So Chief Superintendent, perhaps we could start with you and find out all about matters from your perspective, and then we can move on to DI Brightwell. I'm so looking forward to hearing about the funeral of dear old Sergeant Boniface; and then Barbara, you can add your pennyworth, which I'm sure will complete the puzzle."

She smiled at them as Monty began.

"So we can assume," she went on after she had listened carefully to all the reports and her many questions had been answered to her satisfaction, "that all is now under control. London is sending down two, possibly three more operatives to 'assist' us; it is only a matter of time before Traffic Warden Parkes is found, and I can now release the delegates in perfect safety from the Winter Gardens conference centre. The PM incidentally, was flown out an hour ago and is back in London at a meeting of COBRA. I actually can't imagine why he has taken matters that far, but you know these politicians. Need to be seen to be doing something by the public and the election is only eight months away. Better safe than sorry eh? So nothing else people? Is that what you are telling me? If there is anything else in the wood pile that you just might think relevant, tell me now. No? Good!" She took up her phone and assured her people at the Winter Gardens that all was safe and that the conference could carry on as normal. She looked at her three visitors, as though for assurance that she had done the right thing.

They all nodded and Monty reinforced his nod with assuring words.

It was just as he was guaranteeing to Liz that everything was fully under control and that the whole thing was overstated in any case, and that there was absolutely no need to maintain a high alert state for the conference and the PM could be assured that all was safe and sound, when Lennie, in the back garden of 39 Northbrooke Avenue, lit his cigarette and flicked his lit match away. A full millisecond later, the glowing head of the match met the house full of gas, which was still emanating from Mrs Parkes's cooker, which had been feeding gas to the area for nearly an hour. In another instant it had blown down what looked like half the street, while at the same time causing the almost total destruction of the largest electrical substation in the city.

As the lights went out around her and her computer turned itself off, Slippery Liz looked out of her office window at the ever growing spiral of smoke and debris that was rising just like the mushroom cloud of an atomic bomb, from just over two miles away, and looked back at her three white faced subordinates. Five minutes later, following a complete, verbal analysis of each of their competencies - or lack of them, and a few more minutes employing one of her special rants, Monty, Dibsey and Barbara shot out of the front door of the County Police HQ, like corks out of a champagne bottle;

each with some very specific instructions rammed into their brains by a very angry Chief Constable.

Chapter Sixteen

"What the bloody hell was that?" exclaimed Reggie in alarm. Reggie, Phyllis and Reggie's mum, involuntarily ducked as a large explosion rocked Shelley Mansions. Reggie shot to the window and looked out at a huge plume of smoke and other bits and pieces rising into the sky about a mile away.

"That's the electricity power station," he exclaimed again. "Bloody hell! My house might be damaged if they've bombed the power station." He tried the lights with no joy. "No lights. It's the power station alright."

"Well the papers did say there was a possibility of terrorist action," said Phyllis mildly. "And it looks like they were right. Bloody people."

What are you two gossiping about?" Cut in Reggie's mum, her laptop working on battery. "That bang? It's them rockets probably. Now where's that password? C'mon you little sucker. Where are you?" She hunched back over the laptop, typing furiously. Reggie and his girlfriend wanted information and information is what they'll get. Bangs and explosions weren't important, whatever Reggie said. He was always going on about something or other and he never knew what he was talking about. Rockets! That's what they were.

"I'm going to have to get over there you know. I can't just stay here and wonder what happened to the house."

"No you bloody well aren't" responded Phyllis sharply. "You stay here. It's dangerous out there. There're terrorists and dodgy police, and armed robbers and real police, and they all reckon you're the terrorist and that you've got their property. Which of course you have. Where do you think you'll get with that lot swilling around in all directions? Prison, that's where. And they'll ask questions later and that'll implicate me and your mum. Now you stay here and shut up, and I'll go and see what's what. They don't know me. And keep your mum company and for heaven's sake find out what's so incriminating on that flash drive while I'm gone."

Reggie turned to his mum and watched her in awe as her fingers flew over the keyboard and as strange things came up on the screen. He knew Phyllis was right. He mustn't risk being seen yet, especially with this terrorist thing hanging over him.

"Operation Sky High. That's what did it Reggie. Sky High. Nice name, but no good to me. Just a list of old names. No cleaning powder in any of them. Stupid file that one. I'll keep looking though, don't you worry. Vacuum cleaner bags don't come into it at all. Stupid things. All those names! I've heard of a couple of them on the telly. Or was it the radio. Reggie, was it the telly or the radio? I can't remember. Reggie. Oh, there you are. Reggie, was it……..?"

"It's OK mum, we'll just wait for Phyllis to get back and then I think I'm going to tell someone where I am." Reggie thought hard. He needed someone he could trust. Someone sensible, who would help him and Phyllis to sort everything out. He needed help with this flash drive to find out what was on it, and also, he was getting a bit frightened about everything. The thought that Phyllis could get hurt suddenly popped into his mind and he realised that possibly for the first time in his life, he was worried about someone other than his mum. It was a nice feeling, if a bit scary. He sat back and waited for Phyllis.

Lennie realized his error with cigarette and lighter, a mere nanosecond before his world blew up. The off smell! Of course; it was gas! But his moment of absolute clarity about the matter at hand was snuffed out quickly, as the air beside him became a raging inferno and one of the sides of the coal bunker fell in on him and pinned his right arm to the ground. He was extremely lucky to be alive. Having ducked down behind the concrete coal bunker to get out of the wind and light his cigarette, much of the blast had gone over and round him, rather than through him as it would have done if he had still been standing near the back door. True, the near wall of the bunker had fallen on his right arm, breaking it and pinning him to the ground, but as he had fainted anyway, it was of no worry to him at all.

His boss, Salim had fared far worse. He had almost reached the corner of the road and was actually in sight of the car when he looked round in total horror at the fireball winging its way down the street towards him at high speed. The flames didn't actually reach him as he fled towards the car, because of the hedges and trees between him and the source of the explosion, but the blast did with unbelievable force and blew all his clothes off before bowling him over and rolling him along the ground. Almost into the path of a white police van.

"Look! Over there! That bugger that was running from the explosion." Shouted Dave. "Look, he's heading to that car. Come on Jan, get the bastard. He looks like he's foreign." Jan flung the van into reverse, did a neat and fast three point turn and raced towards the grey Mercedes parked up the street. "Can't imagine why the sod's naked she shouted. Nice arse though. Shame I can't see the front. Those Foreigners are well known for the size of their….."

"Yeah, yeah, OK Jan," cut in Dave. "Let's just concentrate on getting the bugger shall we." For some reason he felt himself going red at the thought of Jan looking at a man's privates, and began to look at her anew. He hadn't thought of Jan before as anything other than another Traffic Warden, but now, with this new intimate talk of naked men and things, his thoughts were in a state of flux. Jan looked over at him and nodded an OK, and in that one look, Dave realised that she was more than just another Traffic Warden. She was also a bit of a looker.

"Salim, in shock and in a state of absolute panic, and stark naked except for his socks and shoes which for some reason hadn't been touched by the blast, reached the car, reached under the rear and grabbed the magnetic box with the spare keys in it. Fumbling and cursing fluently in both Arabic and English, he managed to open the door and leap in. The Merc raced off like a boy racer as his instincts took over the direction of his body and the car flew down the street.

"I'll get that terrorist sod" shouted Jan, and switching as many lights, bells and sirens as she could, she roared off after the Mercedes. "Hold on Dave. We're gonna have some fun here. Just think! Traffic Wardens capturing a terrorist. How cool is that?"

Salim saw the van as it turned and began to follow him and again he reacted instinctively. He was coming to a bit and began to realise his own predicament. There had been an explosion. The power station had blown up. He was in the vicinity and he had run away from the scene and had been seen by a police van crew running from the scene, and he was an Arab. An Arab running from the scene of an explosion of a major public utility did not look good. And even worse, he was naked and had no identification whatsoever. None of it was a good look and he knew he would face many hours of hell if he was caught before matters were cleared up. He decided that there was no alternative but to outrun the van. And that, he thought, would be easy. But there again, he hadn't reckoned on Jan.

Salim knew he had to keep twisting and turning until his Mercedes was hidden from the people in the van, and then, at his leisure, he could work out a devious route out of the area. Lennie's map was on the passenger seat and his car cleaning overalls were in a bag on the back seat. They'd be a bit short, but he couldn't give a stuff about that. He was naked! Had he known what was going on in Shelley Mansions as he passed the building, he would have stopped, naked or not and done some minor violence on the inmates. Instead, he turned right into Saunders Close and immediately again into Brent Crescent and then onto the Dimchurch Road. The last he saw of the van was in Saunders and he was sure he'd outrun it. Then, worrying more about being naked than staying ahead, he turned off into a side street surrounded by small factory buildings and stopped to put on the overalls.

"We've lost him," said Jan despondently. "I thought I could keep up, but he's just disappeared."

"No he hasn't," said Dave quickly. "Look, any road going in that direction is going to lead onto the Christchurch road in the end. Just get there and I reckon we'll pick him up again."

Jan looked round relieved. Dave was right and she shot down Connaught and onto the main road. "You're right," she shrieked. "There's the shit parked off Grey Street." She rocked the van down the slip road at high speed and did a beautiful swerve turn into the small street. The Merc started moving immediately, shooting off at speed.

"Ram the bastard", shouted Dave. "Go on Jan, ram him. Quick!"

Jan swerved the van across the road, still moving faster than the accelerating Merc and crossed back right across its front, knocking the powerful car against the factory wall. But despite the screeching of metal and the burning of rubber, the Merc kept going and tried to cross away from the van and make its escape.

"No you don't matey," shouted Jan. "Dave, hold on tight. Seat belts and have faith in the airbags." She accelerated rapidly, overtook the Merc, pulled the handbrake on, spun the van round 180 degrees and drove head on into the Mercedes. With an explosion of airbags and radiators, the two vehicles stopped dead. Pushing the bag aside, Jan raced out of the driver's seat, wrenched the door of the Merc open, dived in and less than 30 seconds later appeared at the van door holding a still naked and very shell shocked Salem in an arm lock.

"Quick Dave, those wire ties, Round his wrists like handcuffs. Dave grabbed the tube of ties and whipping one out wrapped it round Salem's wrists. Jan was beaming.

"I told you so didn't I Dave? About what some foreigners are best known for I mean!"

Dave leant into the Merc and pulled out the overalls that Salem had been attempting to get into just second earlier.

"Spoil sport!" Said Jan. She dragged her gaze from Salem's body as Dave pulled up the overalls and said, "the next trouble is though, the van won't work. I only hope Barbara won't get too angry. She said she'd kill me if I crashed it."

"Yeah, but remember, we have caught a dangerous terrorist who's just blown up the electricity of the city, and a few houses from what I could see. I don't think she's going to worry about a van. I'll radio for a lift and I reckon it'll take less than a minute for the police to be here once I tell them who we've caught." Dave was right about that last bit at least.

Jennifer Johnson couldn't believe her luck. With most of her available colleagues and just about every other reporter and journalist in town covering the unexpected events at the party conference in the Winter Garden, the editor had shot out of his office and asked her why the hell she wasn't attending the scene of the explosion already and to take his car and get the hell out there now. He flung the keys of his new Mini Cooper S at her, told her to piss off immediately and disappeared back into his lair. OK, she thought, he's a bit of a miserable shit but at least she was getting a major piece of the action. And in a souped up Mini Cooper S! As she drew near to the devastation she had seen and photographed a naked definitely foreign looking man running from the scene; a police van setting off in hot pursuit of the same naked man who had raced off in a Mercedes, and had witnessed and photographed the devastation at the scene as well as the arrival of the emergency services. As the only reporter on the scene that early in the proceedings, her interview with the senior police official as well as the chief fire officer were hers for the taking, as was the opinion of the county chief engineer with his views on the destruction of the substation. By the time any other reporters arrived, the services were far too busy to talk and she had her scoop well and truly on its way to print in the evening edition of the paper.

Chapter Seventeen

Phyllis approached the area of devastation very cautiously. She was unable to get too near because barriers had been erected around the whole area but she did manage to chat to a young policeman manning one of the service vehicle entrances.

"It's bad in there." He told her. "Five houses destroyed and most of the substation as well. The houses were derelict awaiting improvement except one, so no one hurt, but the electricity is out over most of the town and so far it looks like terrorism. An Arab guy was seen running away from the blast. Starkers apparently! Must have been one of those suicide things gone wrong they reckon. These party conferences are more a problem than anything else. They seem to attract all the crazies, and now terrorists. It's a miracle that no one was killed."

"So no-one injured?" Phyllis asked.

"There was one poor guy badly injured in the garden of number 39, but no one else was around thankfully. Not sure what he was doing there. He was pinned down by one side of a concrete coal bunker by all accounts."

The arrival of another fire truck wanting access through the cordon interrupted the constable's flow, and Phyllis gave him a cheery wave and drove off. She couldn't really work out the exact details in her mind of what was going on, but it seems that ever since Reggie got hold of that package she gave him, he had been attracting trouble. And now even his house had been blown to smithereens. She realised it was his house they were after and not the power station, but it would be no good telling the police that. Even if they did take any notice, they'd ask her how she knew. No! Best just to get back and report things to Reggie and then work something out. The whole thing was getting too big to sort out on their own, but who to trust? Reggie was in real trouble, and the authorities of one sort or another would soon find him. And she was sure that there was another agenda out there forcing the issue. He was only a Traffic Warden and was disposable. Then the idea hit her. The Traffic Wardens! OK, they were filth of the first order of course, fit only for the firing squad, but they tended to stick together. After all, they'd put up with Reggie all these years. She had no illusions about Reggie, but he was a decent man at heart and the way he looked after his mum and his chinchillas defined him in many ways. Yes, the Traffic Wardens would somehow have to be brought in to help. They wouldn't let down one of their own, surely? It was too late now anyway, she thought worriedly. There was no help anywhere else. The full weight of the law and even senior politicians seemed out for Reggie's blood. Her thoughts were confirmed as she passed the minimarket just down from Shelley Mansions, and saw the newspaper bill boards screaming out their new message.

TERRORISTS STRIKE AT THE VERY HEART OF BRITISH DEMOCRACY
Exclusive Report by Jennifer Johnson

A naked Arab looking man was seen fleeing the scene of devastation in Westbourne today in what seems to have been a suicide bombing attempt gone wrong. Pursued by a police van manned by Traffic Wardens, which was at the scene, the man raced off in a Mercedes Benz but was caught in a road off the Dimchurch expressway and is now being interviewed by police. All available fire service vehicles ... ...

SUSPECT BOMB FACTORY DESTROYED IN BLAST
Special report by Jennifer Johnson

Police are still attempting to trace a missing Traffic Warden, Reggie Parkes whose house was destroyed in the blast, and who may have been an accessory to the atrocity carried out in the city today. Thought to be associated with terrorism, Traffic Warden Parkes, who earlier this year bravely foiled a suspected jewel robbery, but has since become embroiled in the shady world of terrorism and the arms trade, was last seen ……………………….

TERROR OUTRAGE PLUNGES PARTY CONFERENCE INTO DARKNESS. POLICE AND ARMY ON FULL ALERT
By our senior reporter at the scene, Jennifer Johnson

Raids were carried out at suspect households across the South of England in the last hour as police and the intelligence services reacted to today's bombings in the Southern seaside town of Westbourne. Emergency services were called at 10 O'clock this morning to attend the aftermath of the bombing of the electricity substation in Northbrook Road. The Chief Fire Officer for the County told me that…………………………

This is not a good look thought Phyllis as she purchased a couple of the papers. Now everyone will be against Reggie and we're going to need help more than ever. She drew up at Shelley Mansions, and opened the door of the car, bumping an elderly man who had been walking past carrying some bags of shopping. The shopping scattered all over the pavement as she went to help him pick everything up. "I am sorry mister." She told him, picking up an onion. "I was preoccupied with something else and I just didn't see you. I'm really sorry"

She felt into the gutter to get some rogue apples. The man got down to look under the car for errant apples and onions and looked up at her. "Please don't concern yourself madam." A cultured voice.

"No one's hurt, but if you could help me up, I'd be grateful. It's my knees you know. If I get down, it takes ages to get back up again." Phyllis gladly helped him up, made sure he had all his shopping safely back in the plastic bags and saw him on his way, thinking how nice it was every now and again to meet nice people. People who wouldn't immediately want someone to blame for every little accident. And cultured too! But suddenly remembering her mission, she glanced up and down the street just to make sure no one was looking at her, and strode up to the door.

Reggie looked gloomily at the papers. "They're worse than the last lot. Oh Phyllis what the bloody hell are we going to do. Mum's babbling on about those rockets again and we're getting nowhere really and now everyone thinks I'm a terrorist. And what with the house being blown up, I'm going to have to give myself up you know because……"

"You'll do no such thing Reggie Parkes," cut in Phyllis sternly. "Now have this scotch to settle your nerves and sit down. I've got a plan. It might not work though as it depends on your mates sticking by you, but at least it's a plan and it can't be as bad as just sitting here doing nothing but worry."

"What mates?" Said Reggie. "I haven't got any mates. Only mum! Oh, and now you and Muggins of course." Reggie shuddered slightly at the thought of Muggins and those ghastly bulging eyes being a mate, but he was getting used to change these days and Muggins was all part of it. "Deidre in the Pig might be a mate. I'm not sure. She listens to me though and that's mates isn't it?"

Phyllis's eyes raised skywards. He really didn't have a clue. "Yes you have got mates Reggie. You've got the rest of the Traffic Wardens and…….."

"Don't make me laugh Phyllis. That load of piss taking sods wouldn't support me. I get on their nerves. I know that, so don't try and pretend……….."

"Reggie. Now listen to me. You're being a prat. Everyone out there is after your blood and after seeing the devastation in your road; no one's going to have any mercy on you, because they all think you're a part of it. To them, you're a bloody terrorist. Those Traffic Wardens are your only help and if I'm right, and I am generally right by the way, they'll help. Now how to get in touch with them is the question."

For some reason, Reggie felt easier when he heard Phyllis talking that way. Perhaps they would help. At least they'd listen to him which is more than the police would do. In the very short time he had known Phyllis he had generally found her views on matters were sound. And if she was a bit forceful, it was generally for his own good. Anyway, with half the world on his back, he knew he really didn't have much choice.

"Yes, you are probably right Phyllis. I can't use my police radio to contact anyone, 'cos everyone will hear that, but I've got a list of mobile contact numbers that we have to carry around. Hold on a minute, it's in my room." Reggie stopped as the realisation hit him that he didn't have a room anymore, and anyway, he wasn't at home. "Shitty death! I forgot. I tell you Phyllis, this whole thing is sending me round the bend." He sat down wearily at the kitchen table.

Could it be in your phone Reggie? The number for one of them. Any of them. Phyllis looked at him despairingly. Did you phone any of them recently?"

Reggie started. "No, I haven't called any……No wait. I did. I called Dave to let him know I wouldn't be in early, the other day. Bloody 'ell! Was it really only the other day? Seems like centuries ago. Hold on." Reggie fumbled with his phone, his fingers stumbling over themselves in his anxiety, and by the time Phyllis had nearly passed out with frustration at his slowness, he dialled Dave's number.

"I'm still not sure about this Phyllis, but I suppose you're right. No one else is going to help. He looked round at his mother who had fallen fast asleep across the laptop, and wondered for the millionth time that day just how he had got into this mess. It's just one bloody thing after another, he thought glumly, but there again……"Ah Dave? Dave it's Reggie; Reggie Parkes here. You remember me, don't you? Have you got a moment?"

Chapter Eighteen

Brigadier Archie Fitzpaine stared gloomily out of his grubby window overlooking the back of Kensington Barracks. There was so much pigeon shit on the glass, he was surprised it didn't fall out under the strain. But pigeons were the last thing on his mind at that moment. His world was crashing down around his head because of the antics of a bunch of Traffic Wardens, and as each new solution to the problem came into sight, it was ripped away almost by… well in fact he couldn't work out why. It almost seemed like some sort of juju. He knew about Juju. His time in Nigeria in the old colonial service just before independence had opened his eyes to many weird things, and when he learned that a the local village witch doctor had regularly put spells on his men to stop them investigating crimes, he himself had been prevented from sorting it all out by the threat of particular nasty spell involving a very private part of him shrivelling up and falling off. Perce Smith and now Salim, and Stan and Lennie, all first class operators, but all out of action as if by magic and he wondered if there were any Nigerians in the Traffic Warden outfit. His main worry at the moment though was Salim. Caught stark naked and with no identification whatsoever, in a street by a female Traffic Warden - he shuddered at that thought. Salim was now being held by the Westbourne Police as a terrorist suspect and seemingly no amount of telephone diplomacy seemed able to obtain his release. How the hell Salim had got himself into that mess God only knew. He was usually so spot-on in things. So precise and reliable. Nothing went wrong with Salim. Archie only knew about his predicament in the first place when he recognised Salim from the unfortunate photo given out on the news, and he immediately realised its implications. Foreign looking; naked; bomb; terrorism; fleeing the scene; no ID and so on. Not a good look for the man at all. He'd still got one good man down there, blending in to the local scenery, but what could one man do against these juju maniacs, when experts had failed.

'Oh well,' he thought, 'Salim will just have to sweat it out for a while.' He was a worry, but his main priority was to retrieve that bloody flash drive and that meant finding that bloody Traffic Warden at any cost. The PM wanted that drive, and the PM would get that drive. His own boss the Home Secretary had said so. Desperate he sounded. There must be something very important on it for all this fuss, but that was what his little group was for, sweeping problems under the carpet and keeping them there, so he'd better come up with something quick. He still wondered how it could all have gone so wrong though. He picked up the phone and called his second in command. He had decided that the effort must be stepped up. More manpower and better leadership in the field. In other words, he would have to lead the team in situ, and the team would flood the town. Shock and Awe! He liked that American term, even though his outfit had to blend into the local scenery and do it all in secret and no one was meant to know that they were being shocked and awed. Failing miserably to work out the contradiction of those two statements and unable to sit still for more than ten seconds because of the stress of it all, Archie decided to collect his deputy and sweep her out of the building and into the Grenadier in Belgrave Square for a planning meeting with essential accompaniments. Bloody hell did he need a drink. But as he left the office carefully closing and locking the door, his mobile phone rang.

At that exact same moment, Dave's phone also rang. Dave and Dan were fed up. Jan crashing the third van had cheered them up a bit, but as they were back with Dan on foot patrol and the novelty of walking around all over the place without a van was beginning to pale. In fact, if truth be told, it had paled the instant they had reported for duty.

For the millionth time that morning, Dan looked at Dave and said, "I'm bloody fed up wi' this crap."

"Hold on a mo Dan, I'll just get this call." Dave pulled the mobile out of his pocket and his eyes opened in surprise. "Reggie, is that you? Dan, it's Reggie" he added in a whisper. "On the phone," he added just in case Dan imagined Reggie to be communicating telepathically. "Come over here!" He turned back to the phone.

"Reggie? Are you in a bit of trouble? Have you been blowing things up and the like?"

"Course I'm in trouble and no, course I haven't bloody well blown anything up. I know all about blowing things up, don't you worry. I've got a wound. You don't have to tell me about blowing things up. In fact if you want to know….." Phyllis prodded him hard in the ribs and with a start, Reggie recovered himself. It was always the same with these bloody Traffic Wardens. He always went into mega defensive mode when he spoke to them, the piss taking bastards. He carried on hurriedly.

"Well anyway Dave, forget all that for a minute will you. Listen carefully. Don't tell anyone that I've contacted you yet. Just you and Dan, get over to Shelley Mansions. Along Knightsbank Parade through the underpass. Top floor, number seven. Got it? Oh, and bring Keith. That's important. Do you know where I mean?"

"Yeah, I know where it is. Area 8. See you soon as. Not sure when Reggie but we'll be there a s a p. But where the hell have you ……." The phone went dead. Dave put it back in his pocket and looked worriedly at Dan. "He wants to see us at 7 Shelley Mansions, with Keith!"

Dan looked at Dave and they both nodded. "Barbara is going to have to know this Dave. If the Traffic

Wardens are going to help Reggie, then all of us are going to have to be in on it. It won't work otherwise. You know that."

"Yeah, I know. Well, I vote we go get Keith and then go and see Barbara and leave it in her hands."

They both plodded off towards police central and Dave gave Keith a radio call asking him to return to base. Dan returned to his usual topic of grumbling, the lack of the van was still hurting badly, especially his feet.

"All this bloody walking is getting me down you know. I'd love to get that van back, but now Jan's crashed the latest, we haven't got one at all. No way are the police going to give us another one. And what a van that last one was! Did you see those lights? Course, that was you and Keith fighting over the seat like a couple of kids that got us into that trouble in the Pig that started all this."

Dave looked away guiltily. He knew the fault lay in his stubbornness and unspoken rivalry with Keith over seniority, but Keith was no less to blame and anyway, what's done is done, and he consoled himself with the thought that they'd at least keep fit. "Did you see the look on Deidre's face though Dan? It was almost worth it, just to see that." He laughed at the thought.

"Yeah, there was that to it." Admitted Dan, grinning despite himself. "Mind you Dave, we three must have looked a right load of prats sitting there, looking directly at Deidre, like three wise monkeys; especially as

Keith was sitting on your lap at the time. No wonder Deidre went into shock." They both laughed at the thought.

"It's going to be interesting seeing Reggie again. You know, after all this funny business and us not knowing what the 'ell's going on like. Word has it that he keeps chinchillas."

"What are they when they're at home?" replied Dave, not really interested in the details of chinchillas, but idly keeping the conversation going.

"Not sure really, I did hear they are a sort of cross between a rat like thing and some other thing with big ears," replied Dan vaguely, like Dave, losing interest in the conversation, "but I'm not too sure."

"What, sort of like a squirrel or something?"

"No dumbo! A squirrel's a squirrel, isn't it! It's an animal on its own like. And anyway, I don't think you can keep squirrels. They're more wild type things. They eat nuts and stuff like that and climb trees. You can't just keep them at home in a cage."

"I meant size wise and in looks," retorted Dave hotly. "I didn't mean squirrels were crossed with rats or anything, and I know they're just squirrels and anyway, fancy thinking I'd think like that you great oaf and if……….."

They walked on arguing, their humour gradually decreasing in direct proportion to their proximity to the police station, until soon and in silence, they were grimly and silently trudging up the station steps and through the great front door.

"Ok, you three, this had better be good, because I'm bloody busy arranging tasks for each and every one of you to help with this terrorist business and the Reggie thing. Jan's wrecked the new van and brought in a naked prisoner whom we don't know what to do with, and if we don't find Reggie soon, the Chief Super is going to eat me alive."

Dan, now feeling a lot better knowing about Jan's part in the destruction of the super van, dropped the bombshell.

"Reggie's contacted us Barbara. He wants help. The feeling is that we ought to give it to him. There's something odd going on here and I reckon we are the only ones who can sort it out. Anyway, can you really imagine Reggie as a terrorist?"

All Barbara's thoughts of being busy arranging tasks for everyone, went out of the window on hearing this information and she wasn't at all sure whether it was welcome news or not. She wanted Reggie where he was meant to be, in police custody. That would end her problems and life in the Traffic Warden department could continue in peace and contentment for all. But she also knew in her heart of hearts that Dan was right. Reggie was no terrorist. A bloody nuisance, yes. A complete pain in the arse, yes, but terrorist? No. Definitely not. He wasn't half smart enough. She knew though that if she and her crew were to help Reggie, and she was found to be perverting the course of justice; Dibsey and the Chief Super would have no mercy on her, and all her future plans of getting her pension and retiring to a little croft on South Uist would be dead in the water.

"Right Dan. Get round to his place, or whoever's place it is and invite him to visit me in my office. Tell him that he can bring whoever he is with and tell him to do it fast before someone else catches him and sticks him on a terrorism charge. You know what'll happen then. They'll throw away the keys. And by the way, tell him that we're on his side. It'll keep him happy for a while at least, until I can decide what's to be done. Anyway, go get him now."

Chapter Nineteen

James Arbuthnot was finally satisfied. He had watched Shelley Mansions for a day now and the tiny bug that he had secreted on Mrs Elworthy's person during the shopping incident was producing results. By asking the hospital that had accommodated Reggie during his hero period for a list of visitors, James had, by a series of eliminations and deductions, worked out that the Mrs Elworthy could possibly lead him to Reggie. Obtaining her name from the hospital visitor register for those injured patients under police protection, he had soon managed to find her address, and from there, the rest was easy. The bug had now stopped operating for some reason, but that didn't matter. He had found Reggie, and all he had to do now was tell his boss.

When Archie Fitzpaine heard the news of Reggie's location from James, his disappointment at not being able to take his deputy to the Grenadier disappeared in an instant. He knew that putting a silent operative into the field, unknown to the others, could be the key to the quest, and he had been right. And, he thought, elderly men like James are a threat in no one's eyes. Polite, old fashioned courtesy and being well spoken passed easily with them and didn't stick out at all. They are invisible. They make some of the best agents. Now, he could sort the matter out in no time. It would only take a few men, he thought.

About four should do the trick, and he himself would lead them. No harm in showing his superiors his mettle in the field. Especially as it was already a done deal. So instead of gazing into the eyes of his lovely deputy in the Grenadier, he put such delicious thoughts aside for a later time and began to organise his little field operation. By two O'clock, he was in the car heading South with four of his best men.

As soon as Reggie leaves the building, he thought, he and his men would be in. James could be trusted to delay Reggie's return somehow if necessary, and in the meantime, his men would carry out a forensic search of Mrs Elworthy's flat in Shelley Mansions. There would be no mistakes this time. They would find the package.

DI Brightwell was also in a fairly chipper mood that morning. He had an operation to plan. An operational plan that would show beyond all doubt that he, Dibsey, was composed of the right sort of steel that would gain him promotion. He knew, as did everyone else, that the Chief Super was on the point of either promotion or handing his notice in and looking forward to a long retirement at the nineteenth hole, and either way, he, Dibsey was the one to fill his boss's shoes. There would be no mistake about that after the little surgical strike that he was busy planning. No mistake at all. In his post operational report, he would generously mention the input of WPC Katy Knipe, who had seen Mrs Elworthy's red Lada with what looked like a Traffic Warden sitting in the front passenger seat and had mentioned this fact in her detailed, daily report. The lovely WPC Knipe prided herself on her reports which were always extremely accurate and detailed, and although she hadn't realised the significance of her sighting, she did know that the car had shot through a traffic light which was decidedly pinkish, if not totally red. She had carefully noted the number plate down and written in her notebook; 'Red Lada, plate number, female driver, Traffic Warden passenger, elderly woman in back seat right hand side'. The rest was, as they say, history. Dibsey now knew where Reggie was hiding and he made his plans accordingly.

The modus operandi of James Arbuthnot and his team was based on discretion. Merging into the background and becoming visible only when absolutely necessary. They would get noisy and fight if they had to but not until then. That's where he reckoned his lieutenants had gone disastrously wrong in their attempts to find Reggie and the package. Stan getting his fingers broken in a door! Lennie in hospital with a badly broken arm and minor burns, and Salim; well, best not go there. God only knew how Salim had got himself into such a pickle. Running naked down a street chased by a female Traffic Warden! Like many others, he shuddered at the thought. But now was his moment. His team slipped quietly over the fence at the back of the small area of weedy grass that the owners of Shelley Mansions liked to refer to as its 'extensive grounds'. They crouched to the ground and stayed still. Blue One detached himself from the group and moved round to the front to recce the situation. Archie thought it a bit melodramatic, but there again, what was the point of being seen when there was no need to be seen? One never knew what the future would bring and in this day and age when covert operations tended to enter the public domain in the courts, it was best to be discreet at all times. The torch signal from Phyllis's flat confirmed to him that all was well. As his watcher James had said, the occupants were out and the flat was ready for inspection of a most detailed nature. Seconds later, the team began to search the premises.

The modus operandi of Dibsey and his team was based on making their police presence felt in a most definite way. Shock and Awe! Noise! Get in their face was his motto. Let them know who and what you are, snatch Parkes and anyone with him and don't take any shit. With this in mind, he had planned his raid on Shelley Mansions accordingly. Terrorism and terrorists didn't have rights as far as he was concerned and knocking on the door was therefore not an option for him. The door broke after just one thump from the door smasher, hefted by a large constable who closely resembled a heavyweight boxer Dibsey had known earlier in life. He knew the terror group was in the flat because he could hear them. True, they were quiet, but there was movement within and Dibsey decided to wait no longer.

"Everyone freeze, you're all under arrest," screamed Dibsey as they rushed in through the door and burst into the small sitting room come kitchen come lounge area. The noise of his policemen shouting was suddenly drowned out by a single shot, fired by Archie, more in panic than anything else. He was buggered if he was going to be killed by terrorists, and if it meant killing them outright, who the hell was going to worry. Certainly not the PM, or the great British public who were totally fed up with the bastards. Backing away and falling over the magazine rack as he fired, Archie's bullet rocketed through the stem of the large fan hanging from the ceiling; Phyllis's pride and joy, broke off its mooring and landed smack on the head of Constable Jones as he rushed through the room in search of the terrorists.

Dibsey and the rest of his men dropped and stayed low behind the large lounge sofa. He had thought about firearms use and was ready. "Move in Alpha. Move in Alpha. Go Go Go!" shouted Dibsey into his radio, absolutely delighted to be able to call in the CO19 Force Firearms Unit waiting outside at the back of the building. This was movie stuff. Hero stuff. Thank God he had planned this thoroughly he thought, wiping his brow. Controlling his own SWAT team, or as near a SWAT team you could get in the UK. These boys will get the terrorists and if Reggie goes down, so be it. Silly beggar, getting involved in terrorism.

"Friendlies behind the sofa, one friendly lying across the dining room table with a fan on his head; terrorist suspects in bedrooms and kitchen," went on the radio operator, giving instructions and directions to the heavily armed CO19 team. That was another thing thought Dibsey. Good old fashioned radios. They always worked.

Over the next few seconds, Dibsey and his men marvelled at the sheer fluidity and precision of the armed police team as they entered the flat and began their work of tracking down the terrorists. But then matters began to go pear shaped. Within minutes he got a tiny inkling that matters were not all going CO 19's way. The flat was too tiny to manoeuvre adequately and the carefully practised choreography of the team became a bunched-up mass of men jammed into small corridors and totally unable to manoeuvre. And to make matters worse and adding to the jam, the terrorists weren't fleeing. They were fighting back and already one heavily armoured police man was lying on the floor holding his leg and being trampled by all the others. A cupboard full of tea towels above the stove, the subject of a keen search by one of Archie's men, had disgorged its contents and with the stove ring evidently on for some reason, was beginning to smoke.

Dibsey looked at the scene over the back of the sofa in alarm. "OK lads," he yelled at his men, emerging from behind the sofa. "We're going to have to help. Oh, and radio for an ambulance soonest," he ordered. Glancing around the room, he saw flames flicker from the kitchen stove, which seemed to have been left burning, but he was too busy launching himself at the enemy to worry about it at that moment. He couldn't see Reggie anywhere but he flung himself at the terrorist who seemed to be giving the orders and wrestled him to the ground. Archie, unable to bring his gun to bear in the confines of the tiny kitchen dropped it and desperately tried to kick off the overweight lout who had landed on him and who thankfully seemed unable to kick him back because he was jammed up against the wall. The whole flat seemed now a mass of men trying to fight each other, but encountering a million different obstacles in their quest for personal destruction, such as tables and sofas and beds and toilets and a million other things.

The noisy arrival of the ambulance teams only made matters worse, and oblivious to the fighting or rather what had become a pushing and shoving match, the ambulance paramedics did their best to evacuate the one policeman and one terrorist from the tiny loo who seemed somehow to have slipped and hit his head on the toilet pan.

"Oi!" Shouted the chief paramedic. "The bloody place is on fire you buggers. For God's sake, put the flames out. Daisy. Call the fire brigade or we'll all end up roasted."

Daisy, who had been wiping blood from the head of the toilet terrorist, quickly radioed for help from a fire team and carried on with her messy job, ducking her head as a terrorist swung his arm at a policeman. And the smoke kept coming.

Dibsey and Archie looked up in alarm as more and more, thick, black smoke began to fill the flat and as flames began to lick around them, and the flat fire alarms started their frantic beeping, the urge to fight and kill; or at least badly maim, left them, and was superseded by a desire to get out.

Within minutes, the fight to the death between two groups of deadly enemies had become a fight to get out of the flat to safety and just as the ambulance team managed to get the two wounded onto stretchers and raise them up on their telescopic legs, the rush to get out became a stampede, knocking the stretchers and their injured occupants flying. The rest of the occupants of the Mansions were already outside looking dazed at the scene unfolding before them.

The scene outside Shelley mansions was equally chaotic. James's men and Reggie's policemen as well as CO19, the ambulance crew and the other occupants of the mansions were rushing to escape from the by now well burning building, while the fire crew were running in the opposite direction, equally determined to get in. When the two groups met, the new chaos became truly ugly. But in the midst of it all, James shouted rapid orders to his men. "RV 10, RV 10. Go Go Go. His men ran, each of them in a different direction, but each heading in a roundabout way to rendezvous number 10; a disused boiler house in Ealing, where they could recover and recuperate, and no doubt be given the bollocking of their lives.

"Shit" said Dibsey as he watched them go. He knew it would be no good trying to get his men to chase them; they were knackered beyond belief and choking their lungs out, lying all over the grass and in any case, the CO19 boys had leapt into their big black van and had disappeared.

Jennifer Johnson, rapidly rising star of the newspaper world snapped away happily at the scene before her. Being the keen young reporter she was, she had followed the ambulance to the scene, just in case there was a story at the end of it. Having lost it several streets away, she picked up the trail when the fire engines sped past her. And here she was. Reporting on an armed battle between the police and a group of deadly terrorists, with the gallant fire and ambulance crews doing their duty in the midst of it all. Her joy knew no bounds, and her scoop would sell newspapers for weeks - and of course keep her own shooting star in the ascendancy. True, her request for an interview with Detective Inspector Brightwell whom she had seen standing outside the inferno gloomily watching the blaze, had resulted in her being told to 'fuck off,' ditto the chief paramedic who went further and suggested she 'go stick her head up her arse and choke', but that was life as a reporter she supposed, and those comments would be reported. The battle for Shelley Mansions had ended. The building was reduced to bare metallic bones, standing starkly against the dark evening sky.

Dibsey called for his car and returned wearily to the office. He doubted that things could get much worse. He was wrong.

Chapter Twenty

Sir Cuthbert Montgomery, late of Eton and Oxford, and current Home Secretary was a worried man. Cloistered in his office with the Defence Secretary, he was not enjoying the evening. Having been dragged out of his club by a curt order from the PM, and having suffered a restrained but meaningful and very pointed 'interview' at Number 10, he had called in Defence in order to beg, steal and borrow their expertise. The expertise he wanted was that of the SAS. Nothing else would do he thought. He couldn't imagine quite how it had all happened. From what was initially a simple, but urgent job to retrieve a sensitive flash drive, there had developed a chaotic situation of almost global proportions. Certainly, it was being reported around the globe and making the British police and other forces of law and order look stupid beyond belief.

From what he was able to glean from the Chief Constable of the county; a woman he hated, for the simple reason that she had once ditched him when they were in their early twenties; a simple Traffic Warden whom everyone thought was a hero, had turned to terror and working with what appeared to be a shady Middle Eastern organisation obviously bent on revenge for past sins, had organised an incredibly successful bombing campaign aimed at bringing a party conference to a grinding halt and embarrassing Great Britain in the eyes of the world. To make matters worse, his own organisation and the police, had helped to destroy all the evidence that could have helped end the business with a botched raid that had ended with the entire place being burned to the ground. It was all too much. And that drive. He really needed to retrieve that flash drive, and all this was getting in the way. His own men had failed there, under that idiot Archie Fitzpaine. He grimaced. He could do without this sort of thing but in the meantime, in order to get the help of the Army, more especially the SAS, he needed to perhaps embellish the story a tadge.

He pressed on hurriedly. "Look here Harry. It's evidently an Al Qaida operation hitting us down in Westbourne. Highly organised, well-armed and equipped and very well disciplined. Five haven't got a clue who's involved and neither have Six, which just goes to show how sophisticated this bombing operation is. Now some arse has destroyed their HQ and any evidence that we could have gleaned has been totally destroyed. According to the local boys, the terrorists did it themselves after being surprised and the way the house went up there could have been explosives there. They all escaped of course. The whole thing's undoubtedly part of a plan to disrupt the party conference and embarrass us in the eyes of the world and it seems to be working and that's where we come in. The forensic boys are pouring over the site now, but you know how long they take, and there isn't much left to look at anyway because the whole lot is scorched to a cinder. Anyway, we need to be seen to be doing more. Ordinary people could get hurt as well you know, and it's an election year, so that means that ordinary people who are hurt won't want to vote for us, so I really need your cooperation on this. It's all got beyond the capabilities of the police services. In fact, I need the SAS. Now what do you say. The PM is keen as well. In fact, he seemed especially keen! I haven't seen him so animated in years. Something must have frightened him. He hates terrorists. We're going to bring all this up at this evening's COBRA committee meeting, so I thought we'd have a quick bilateral now before we have to go in. You know, both speak from the same book as it were. Common ground etcetera, etcetera! Have you seen the papers by the way?"

Harry Burrows, very recently made defence supremo, looked down at the assorted newspapers lying on the coffee table between them and nodded. He had indeed seen the papers. They were there in front of him and nothing of what they said was good. It did look like a sort of bombing campaign; all the signs were there. But he had a gut feeling that all wasn't what it seemed. A lack of any sort of sophistication? No warnings? Nothing fitted with his previous experiences. He couldn't put his finger on it, but there was something just not quite right, and if anyone, he would know.

Having risen through the ranks from private to full Colonel, and having served in Northern Ireland, the first Gulf war and commanded his own battalion in action in the second, as well as in Afghanistan, he was the only ex-soldier in the government ranks and it was probably this factor that differentiated him from everyone else in Cabinet. But he was new in the job and he felt vulnerable against the long serving and very experienced Home Secretary. That was the other thing. The Home Secretary looked over eager to employ the SAS. Home Secretaries rarely wanted outfits other than their own involved. The police, the Yard, MI5, and other, more shady outfits were all Home Office assets. Not the SAS. He looked up.

"Are you sure about this Cuthbert? I mean, I know what it looks like, but is it really a job for the SAS? Especially before forensics have done their bit. I mean, huge gas build ups and explosions can occur and house fires can be caused by any number of things. Stoves being left on for a start, or just plain gas leaks. And from what the police say, there wasn't much happening until they burst in, and they couldn't identify this Traffic Warden chap as being there anyway. The very fact that Five and Six know nothing about this must say something. I mean, have we really looked at................"

"Harry," cut in Cuthbert quickly, sensing that his SAS idea was about to be doubted by no less that the Secretary of State for Defence himself, however new he was. "My dear chap. What do you mean, stoves and gas ovens? A blast of that magnitude evidently well directed at an important electrical substation couldn't surely have come from a gas oven, and the terrorists' house went up in flames so quickly that it was probably booby trapped! As for Five and Six; old fellow, they seem to know nothing about anything these days. I mean, a few weeks ago everyone was praising this Traffic Warden lunatic for being a hero. We wanted to give him medals! Now look at it all. It turns out he's a terrorist mastermind and he's got a flash drive desperately wanted by the PM. Full of classified information. Five and Six didn't have a clue! No, no, no, we need expertise down there and that can only come from your special chaps. Now, when can they get down there?"

He gave in. "Let me make a call Cuthbert. But don't inform the Police. These men work on their own. No other agency involvement. Got that?"

Slippery Liz was a worried woman. Things were obviously not going well at all in her parish and now she had received the call to London, no doubt to explain herself. It wasn't every day that the Home Secretary himself called her, especially the present one. She shivered as she remembered his groping fingers all over her body after the student's union ball at London all those years ago. She had thought she liked him when they first met. He was good looking, quite charming and obviously well-heeled, and she was a very bright, good looking blonde, heading for a first in law. In fact it seemed a match made in heaven and everyone who was anyone expected that match to end in marriage. Severe doubts began to surface in her mind however after she left Cuthbert in her halls of residence room after an unbelievably uplifting session involving a variety of newly purchased play items, while she nipped out to get a couple of takeaways. With no queue in the local pizza emporium, her mission was accomplished a lot faster than she had envisaged and on her return, she burst into the small room, festooned with brown paper parcels of food, only to see the young Cuthbert pissing in her sink. Spinning round while frantically stuffing his equipment back into his trousers, he managed to spray much of the room and his own trousers, and while zipping up, he fled upstairs to the communal bathroom, leaving Liz to clean up the mess.

That, she later discovered was one of his least disgusting habits, and after a year of an embarrassing, frustrating but extremely erotic 'on off' relationship, there was the inevitable acrimonious break up when she found him naked in bed with a transgender Polish psychology lecturer and his or her two boyfriends. It was hilarious until he asked her to join them. Now the dirty bastard was her boss, but until today they had both studiously avoided direct contact.

She boarded the train to London with a lot of foreboding and spent the ninety minute journey gazing into the middle distance, completely unable to read a word of her new sci-fi novel. Had Waterloo Station not been a terminus, she would have passed right through it.

Chapter Twenty One

Reggie's mum and Phyllis sat gloomily in Barbara's office reflecting on the events of the afternoon and evening. Reggie was worried sick about his terrorist status and fondly remembering those days that seemed like years ago when everyone thought he was a hero; and was even beginning to get nostalgic about his former life as an ordinary Traffic Warden that everyone took the piss out of. Phyllis was worried sick about her flat, and Reggie's mum about rockets and the fact that she may have left the cooker plate on in Phyllis's flat. She'd meant to make a cup of tea, but they'd all been told to move so quickly that she'd got confused. Shouldn't do any harm though, she thought comfortingly. And, she'd got her laptop with the rocket stick sitting comfortably on her lap. Dave and Keith stood by the door to make sure no one else entered and Barbara closed the blinds. None of the other Traffic Wardens were around anyway because Barbara had sent the whole lot out on errands to do with the 'developing terrorist situation', but she didn't want any passing policemen to lock eyes on Reggie until she'd found out what the hell was going on'. She at him looked bleakly.

"OK my boy," she started. "Start talking; oh, and tell me everything. And I mean everything Reggie Parkes, because my job, and your job and several high ranking police jobs all depend on what you're going to say. So the merest hint of a porky and I'll dob you in and it'll be straight to jail you go. OK?"

Reggie looked up, realised how it was to be and started his sorry tale. In fact, it came as a relief to share all this shit with someone else. Someone who might just be able to do something about it all.

"Well, it all began in the underpass near Shelley Mansions, and it hadn't been for that old bag Elworthy, I'd still be alright....." He stopped, realising just what he was saying and darted a fearful look at his dear Phyllis. She winked and grinned back at him. "Go on Reggie. That was then. This is now. You just tell Barbara how it was."

Reggie, emboldened by this fine woman's words and determined not to let her down again, continued his story, being careful not to slag off Phyllis again, and half an hour later he had finished. He looked up at Barbara. "And for the rest, you can fill in all the gaps from the papers. Oh, and Keith has found something in the computer that might tell us more about these terrorist incidents, but I need to go to the water closet. I think I'll be safe there on my own." He got up wearily and headed for the door. Barbara nodded to Dave, who reluctantly followed him.

"So Keith, what have you found?"

Reggie's mum looked up interestedly. "He's real good that one. He got through the code and found more than rockets. There're all sorts of bigger rockets and other things as well. There's even a contract!" He hand went to her mouth as she said the word. She wasn't exactly sure what a contract meant, but Keith had seemed amazed when he found it and had almost been afraid to tell her about it. "Tell her Keith. I'll go to the crew room and put the kettle on."

Barbara looked at Keith, relieved that it was him and not Reggie's mum who would explain the contents of the drive.

"It's a farming equipment catalogue and there's a contract, signed by the PM to sell tractors and irrigation equipment to a foreign party Barbara," began Keith quietly. All nice and above board. But under that, deeper into the file and protected by another password is a contract to sell modern, heavy weapons to one of the most brutal dictators in the world. Anyway, it looks like the contract has also been signed by the Prime Minister himself, but if you look carefully, it looks like the signature has been cut and very neatly pasted into the arms document. But then there's something else altogether because hidden even deeper in the files are a series of pictures showing the same Prime Minister cavorting naked with a bunch of assorted naked teens, admittedly probably all over 16 and all female, but still! Apart from the teenies, there's a radiator, handcuffs, a tennis racket and several multi-coloured balloons involved. Oh, and by the way, one of the girls is Roxy, Reggie's niece. You wouldn't want to see the pictures Barbara, I can tell you."

Barbara, who definitely did want to see the pictures gave a knowing grin, but suggested that it might anyway be a good idea to get everything in print, just in case so that there would be physical evidence that might help Reggie. She would keep the photos safe in her filing cabinet. She'd have to mention the Roxy business and the PM to Reggie, but she'd do it through Phyllis, who looked a woman of the world and would be able to explain it in terms that Reggie would understand. But that could come later because Reggie had just re-entered the room, followed by a very pissed off Dave.

Keith continued. "OK then. But it was bloody difficult to get into those files you know. Some clever bastard hid them behind layers of codes and passwords. But I'll give Reggie's mum her due, she uncovered the first and most difficult layer. All the layers came from downloads which I presume have been destroyed otherwise this stick wouldn't be so important."

"But why send it by post? Why not by email?"

"Because cyber-attacks are occurring more and more frequently these days Barbara. Emails can be easily hacked. You've seen the news. That's why Hilary Clinton is a nobody now and not President of the USA. Emails. Normal post is far safer. Can't be hacked"

"Not in this case though it seems," gasped Barbara. "No wonder the PM wants the damn thing back. But I can't think how this is connected to the terrorist business. Are you seriously saying that all the explosions and shootings are all to do with this?" She paused as the phone rang next to her. She gingerly picked it up.

"Barbara speaking, can I help you?" She paused again. Good God! Any casualties? Bloody hell!" She put the phone down and looked at them all.

"There's been a shoot-out between special units of the armed squad, police, and terrorists at Shelley mansions. Somehow the whole building caught fire during the gun battle and the place has burned to the ground. I really can't imagine why Shelley Mansions was anything to do with it, but no wonder the place went up in flames!"

Reggie looked at Phyllis in horror. Phyllis slumped down even further in her chair. Reggie's mum who had returned with her cup of tea suddenly looked up and said, "the cooker. I bloody knew I'd left it on," and she went silent.

The silence ended after thirty seconds as everyone tried to speak at once.

"Shelley Mansions!" Said Barbara, "is that your place ….."

"The stove……………"

"I knew that stick was a problem, but……………"

"Well, I vote we just………………

"Can't you see just what………………"

"Major balls up all round……….."

"Shitty death……….."

"Quiet everyone", snapped Barbara. "Now look. Firstly, we need to think about this. The building has gone. There's nothing that can be done about that. I'm sorry Reggie, for you and Phyllis and of course for your mum, but we'll see you housed until you're sorted, don't you worry. But as for the rest of it, there could be a whole skip full of shit land on top of us, whatever we do. We've seen what's on that flash drive. Either the PM has been blackmailed, or he's been tricked into the arms contract. Either way, we've got to get him out of the shit if only for Reggie's sake." She looked round at everyone present.

She summed it up for them. "The PM and his government are selling nasty weapons to a brutal dictator, but the PM himself thinks he's signed a document selling them farming equipment. According to Keith, it looks like his signature has been moved onto the arms papers. And so the contract has been signed. The weapons are the latest, so says the catalogue. And the PM is a bit of a perv, with pictures to prove it. Not against the law, but I wonder what his wife - or the country would think of it all? But anyway, this whole thing means shit loads of trouble. Double shit loads. If we go to the police, they'll do a cover up. They always do. Can you imagine Slippery Liz not doing what she's told? She wants to go into politics.

Or the Chief Super? He wants a promotion or a quiet retirement. Or Dibsey? He wants to be the Chief Super."

Her voice got higher at the mention of each of them. "And when they've all done their upward shuffle, modern, lethal, British made weapons will start slaughtering innocent women and children. On the news for a week and then forgotten about. If we don't go to the police, the secret boys will hound all of us to pieces. And I mean that literally. That bloke from London who interrogated Reggie for instance. Even Dibsey didn't like him or his methods. He was probably one of them. He was no copper. Even you said there was something funny about him Reggie. And we can't just get rid of the stick. They'll never believe that. They'll know we've got a copy - or several, even if we haven't. And they will find out, believe me. And then what? We'll never be left alone. And anyway, we should do something about it. Not just accept stuff like this. Now Keith, you say there's a digital copy of a signed contract on the stick. So who'd have the hard copy?"

"There probably won't be one," replied Keith. "Remember Barbara that I was a registry computer clerk at the Foreign and Commonwealth Office before I studied engineering, and some of those dodgy deals were never in hard copy, even in the days when there were no sticks or computers. Verbal agreements then. Some were so hush-hush that you won't hear about them for 30 years, or even more in some cases. No, I doubt there's any other copy, hard or digital. This is it. And we've got it. That's why everyone is so desperate to get hold of it. And it has stuff on it that will keep the PM quiet."

She sat back in her chair, ignoring her piles, and forced herself to calm down. We need a plan. A bloody good plan, because we really need to stop this thing and we're very much on our own. It'll be difficult, but we need a sting operation resulting in the PM being totally on our side. In other words, we need to play up the terrorist business, frighten everyone silly, get the PM down here, and tell him all about it. If we try to tell him up in London, we'll never get through the layers of people in front of him. And anyway, I don't think he would want them all in the picture. Young girls and so on! So we get him down here, frighten him, so he will believe us and reveal all. All agreed?"

They looked at her dubiously, wondering just how she was going to fix all that up, but all the same, they all nodded, looking at her with a new admiration. She went even further up in their estimation when she equally decisively said, "OK then. Keith, recall all the Traffic Wardens. The thing about a Traffic Warden gang is that we can be everywhere and we are expected to be everywhere. They can't and aren't. The other thing is that Dibsey knows this and will need our help, which means we, - or at least I, will be in the know. Now, let's get moving. We've got some planning to do. Keith, give us the complete lowdown on that stick and its codes."

'Oh, and Reggie, you and Phyllis can stay at my sister Jackie's for a few days until we find something more permanent. She's away in the RAF and only uses her flat occasionally. No one needs to know where that is, so lips zipped everyone. Now Reggie, where is Roxy staying? Find her if you wouldn't mind. I need a quick chat with that young lady. She could be very helpful. In fact, she could help save the lot of us."

She sat back in her chair. "But first of all, we need an undercover agent. Now, how do we go about that?"

Chapter Twenty Two

The men who grabbed Reggie's mum off the street, were quiet, fast, and efficient and within seconds, she had disappeared off the face of the earth, together with the book entitled, 'Cracking impossibly difficult computer codes made easy', that she had just borrowed from the main Westbourne public library. This highly efficient disappearing act was closely observed by Polly, who, having quickly snapped the kidnap, and the kidnap vehicle on her phone, sent a swift text with the photo to Jan and Dave who were sitting in Dave's anonymous looking, grey Fiat Uno, just around the corner. Taking a quick glance at the picture, and noting the look of the van and its number plate, Jan pulled away from the curb and began to discreetly follow the vehicle. There had been no discussion on who would drive Dave's car, Dave recognising Jan's superior skills in all things motoring, especially when the going got rough. Not, he thought, that she could do much with a Fiat Uno, but at least it was an inconspicuous looking little car, and hardly one that would scare the SAS. And Dave and Jan knew that it was a SAS operation for the simple reason that Barbara had told them it would be. She had been at the planning meeting with Liz. The Defence Secretary's warning not to let the Police in on the operation had been totally ignored simply because the Home Secretary didn't want another

Blue on Blue incident occurring and vowing the Police to cooperation was easily the best way to avoid this. He thought!

The city had become more like a garrison town in the last couple of days. It still wasn't a 'war zone' although smoke still rose into the air from both Shelley Mansions and the substation. Army units were very much in evidence around the town centre area; a large Daring Class navy destroyer was clearly visible sitting off the coast, and unseen, high in the sky above the city, an AWACS aircraft of the Royal Air Force coordinated the whole of the military effort, and provided guarantees of radar coverage over the whole area and far beyond. None of this hardware was really necessary or of any use, the defence secretary had told the Home secretary, but the public had to be reassured about matters, and this part of the action was just for publicity. The government was taking no risks and the PM had been on the television just the evening before, vowing that Britain and the British people would never bow to the dictatorship of terrorism, however much it cost in blood and money. The conference had been terminated and the MPs and assorted hangers on and the party faithful had disappeared. The various ministers who only visited on and off, were all safely ensconced in their Whitehall offices, and the PM, thankful that everyone was safe, and happy in the knowledge that skilled men and women were closing in on the 'package' and the terrorists, was looking forward to a few dalliances with Roxy in his London pad.

After a bruising encounter with the Home Secretary during which both of them wore fixed smiles and remained icily polite, Slippery Liz returned to the fray very much determined to do several things as soon as she was able. Firstly, she decided to resign and go into politics. Sure, she had first to sort out this current mess before she could honourably resign, but it had long been in her mind anyway. Once in politics, she would rise rapidly through the ranks by being a perfect bitch to everyone except those in command, even if it meant sleeping with the lot of them - male or female, and then she would shaft said Home Secretary in the most painful and humiliating way she could think of once she had reached a point where she was able to do so. She couldn't wait for that day and in the meantime, if any opportunity arose which could help hasten her plans, she would immediately, and without question, take it. He had been a complete bastard to her in his little office chat, even suggesting in the most oblique way possible, that her incompetence had dragged the whole government into disrepute, and that it was obvious that she was unfit to be Chief Constable of the County and had probably only got there by sleeping with most of the local force, and probably half the neighbouring county's force as well. She was livid. It was a total lie; it certainly wasn't as many as half the force, and she certainly didn't cross borders, but it infuriated her nevertheless. She knew very well that her moral compass didn't always point true North, but she was a good cop and had beaten her male colleagues to the job because she was good at it, not just because of a healthy lack of morals on her part.

His smile as he told her of his opinion of her remained fixed and it was all she could do to remain seated and not launch at him, remind him of a few of his least disgusting habits and rip his balls off. However, this would definitely not have furthered her plans in any way, so she had taken the shit, promised to sort out the situation in quick time, and left.

Before any of her personal plans could be implemented however, she needed to sort the whole terrorism business out and do it quickly. She realised that the only way to get it all over with quickly was to get together a task force of her people so that all were acting in concert and with one single aim. No more mistakes at funerals. No more involvement with strange units unless she was totally in the know. No more cone vans in pubs, or naked foreigners running around in all directions. In short, no more stupid cockups. She must find the package and Reggie Parkes. Her new team would liaise with the military forces that had offered help, but the whole thing would be under the control of the civil power as was proper. And in this county, that meant her. Except there was the complication of the SAS. Even a Chief Constable couldn't control them even when they were on her patch.

She sat back in her chair and looked round at the Chief Super, Dibsey, and Barbara, her new terrorist task force, all of whom she had invited to a conference in her office to review the situation and try and think of a response to whatever was happening. Matters were getting serious in her parish, the bastard Home Secretary was on her tail, and she knew she needed allies, and she knew that the only allies around were her own staff, and she could be very sweet indeed when she had to be. She was also aware of a growing suspicion in her own mind and the minds of others that all was not quite what it seemed, and if this was the case, she needed to get to the bottom of it as soon as possible.

Dibsey sat looking at Liz in that bemused way he always did when he was in her presence. He could never ever figure out how she had got to be Chief Constable unless it was all in return for favours laid on in bedrooms around the county, and if that was it, he certainly hadn't benefitted. Like Liz though, he was in a state of fury regarding the force, the army, special branch, the Traffic Warden service, and in particular, that miserable shit Reggie Parkes. But his greater ire was reserved for that devil incarnate, Percy Smythe and his bastard oppo Stan. True, they were both out of it now, but they had been the architect of the entire chain of balls ups that had occurred over the last week. First, there was the business of being fobbed off while Percy interviewed Reggie alone in his, Dibsey's office, having deliberately told him the wrong time. Had Dibsey been present, he would never have released Reggie and the whole matter would have been over in a day. None of the terrorist attacks would have occurred and the whole town wouldn't be seething with military types and all sorts of other troops, spooks and geeks. Then the funeral business; here he went red at the mere thought of that episode, which even though he had attempted to blame everyone else but himself, he had finally admitted that it was entirely his own fault; although he could still happily strangle the vicar and stuff Mrs Bonniface in the same coffin as her husband.

Then his immaculate plan to finally capture the terrorist cell with the CO19 Force Firearms Unit couldn't have ended in up as a bigger balls up. The building destroyed, no trace of any terrorists or Reggie Parkes, a copper with a bash in the head, and a very pissed off fire and ambulance service. The only people who had done anything useful, were a couple of Traffic Wardens in a cone van who had managed to snare a suspicious foreigner racing around naked in a downtown street. And even this had come to nothing after the same terrorist was mysteriously and very quickly released following abrupt orders descending from above. It was all an affront to the dignity of the police force; a descent into a shambles that had no part in orderly police work, and it shamed them all. But again he remembered that it had all started with that bastard Smythe, with an 'e', and as he sat there thinking about it, he vowed to get revenge on him as soon as he could. If any opportunity arose in the meantime, he would take it with no questions asked. But like Liz, he knew when he was in a vulnerable situation and he knew he needed help and assistance from everyone in the room. Even Barbara.

Chief Superintendent Monty Matthews was more in command of his senses. He had carefully reviewed the whole situation in his own slow and methodical way and when he looked at each incident, none of them seemed like very much at all. It was like having a jigsaw where the pieces almost fitted together, but didn't quite. And then when he forced them all together, the whole wouldn't hold together. In fact, he didn't believe that anything was wrong at all. There didn't seem to be a terrorist threat when looked at clinically. Only the papers said there was. However, he had to acknowledge that there were greater brains than his at work up in London. Intelligence experts, spooks of all kinds and no doubt the PM himself were all involved in analysing what could be a complex situation. Because of all this, he was loathe to argue or to push his different views forward because with the support of GCHQ, MI5, MI6 and heaven knew who else, they would know far more of the background than him. If it all settled down, all well and good. If it didn't, and it did turn out to be a major terrorist plot, then again, all well and good. His police would reveal the plot and catch and punish those responsible as per usual. Either way, not too much could happen to him. He had now almost decided that he was going to retire and he was too near an honourable retirement to be much affected. The circumstances of the past few days, and his seeming inability to grasp hold of the detail, and the seeming permanence and inanity of Slippery Liz had convinced him of a preference for retirement over promotion. If it also came with a knighthood, all the better. He felt he deserved one, and so did his dear Doris. Let the County go to hell.

So far, he thought, most of the problem was due to sheer incompetence on everyone's part. Brightwell and his stupid funeral, followed by his idiotic SWAT team idea that had merely destroyed the very evidence of terrorism - or not terrorism that the police needed, and pissed off numerous other people into the bargain. Then there was the Chief herself, Slippery Liz ignoring all the signs of trouble brewing and down playing all the obvious signs, even when they blew up in her face five minutes later and covered all and sundry with shit. And as for the Traffic Wardens, it was becoming farcical. Three cone vans written off! One inside a pub for God's sake, actually up against the bar, another managing to write off a Home

Office car as well as itself, and yet another destroyed after colliding with a Mercedes while its crew ran down a naked man that everyone regarded as a terrorist. Well that had come to nothing. One word from an unknown 'special' unit, via Scotland Yard, and the poor sod was re-clothed and repatriated to London on the spot. There was something definitely odd there, and all in all Monty knew, from donkeys' years in the force, that something definitely didn't smell right about the whole business.

The official message he had received from London about the 'captured terrorist' brooked no argument. It said, without actually saying the words, 'send him back immediately or you will be in so much deep shit that you will drown in seconds.' He sent him back. As for the Traffic Warden though, Monty had a sneaking admiration. The poor sod had been feted as a hero one minute and immediately afterwards had been reviled as a terrorist. Hardly a likely scenario. Overall, Monty was confident that in the end, all of this would be sorted out and he would get his newly sought after retirement and just possibly, his knighthood. And 'Lady' Doris would be happy.

Barbara was probably the most confident member of that particular war cabinet; her confidence based on the fact that she knew exactly what was going on. More or less! She knew that absolutely nothing was as it seemed.

The whole town had wound itself up onto a war footing simply because the PM was a bit of a perv and thought he was selling tractors to foreigners. The truth, an arms sale was good for the GDP of course, but strictly against all the principles set out in the government's own white paper on the subject of arms sales - and probably against numerous treaties signed with European and American allies.

She knew that the robbers that had attacked Reggie had been paid by someone and were trying to retrieve something in that post bag. It seemed from the courts that the robbers were after diamonds and that those diamonds were nothing to do with this present mess. Then, what with one thing leading to another, a completely false story about terrorists had somehow been stoked up by an inexperienced dilly of a cub reporter after the start of the persecution of Reggie by Percy. The presence of the flash drive in the same bag was probably purely coincidental, although she wondered who it was going from and who it was going to. Unfortunately, the address cover had gone up in the flames of Shelley Mansions and according to Reggie it was unreadable anyway.

She knew that she could tell none of this to the assembled company, however tempted she was to do so. And she was momentarily tempted. But who was involved with the arms sale? That was the key question, because someone high up was blackmailing the PM. That was the person she needed to draw out. Her team needed to speak to the PM himself, and that she knew would be impossible in the current situation.

If she simply told the unbelievable truth now, in this meeting, she would be regarded as the 'saviour' and would be able to retire to the Western Isles in peace and contentment. The stick would be returned; PM would not be embarrassed - or divorced, but thousands of children and civilians would be killed, and she would never be able to look at herself in the mirror again - and the PM, a man who had the button on nuclear weapons, would be open to blackmail forever. If she was to retire in peace, she simply couldn't let that happen.

If she did let it happen, all of the bastards involved would maintain the status quo, not for their love of politicians, especially the PM, but for their own benefit and promotion, and any dissension from this line would be crushed. Alternatively, she could also be crushed. Her honourable retirement would not occur and it wouldn't surprise her that with stakes this high, her own future would be a nasty accident and a nice obituary in the local rag. But with a bit of luck, and the skills of her Traffic Warden team, she had a good idea of what she needed to do. She knew she was only here because she ran a large team of invaluable 'eyes and ears' on the ground. The perfect secret intelligence service. Who else had a large team that covered every inch of the town day in day out? Quietly going about their business in full sight of everyone, but unnoticed by anyone. She also knew that it was this very same team that would help her sort it all out. With a bit of luck! Her plan had already started, with the kidnap of Reggie's mum.

"Well ladies and gentlemen" continued Liz, beaming at each and every one of them. "Things seem to have taken a few turns for the worse recently, but I do know that with your collective leadership, loyalty, hard work and innovative ideas, we will soon establish the truth of just what is going on. The Chief Super will head the operational team with Dibs..er, sorry, the Detective Inspector as his deputy, and I rely on you all to do your best. The situation is serious. I can only rely on you good people. Now this is what we are going to do."

It was then that she informed her loyal team that the SAS, working closely with the Scotland Yard anti-terrorist unit, MI5, MI6 and GCHQ, would kidnap Reggie's mum. "That will draw him out from wherever he's hiding. We've profiled our man, and he'll do anything for his mum. We have received information from London that prior to the terrorist incidents, his gang stole a flash drive from a government courier containing highly sensitive, secret information that could adversely affect our ability to fight the war on terror or whatever they are calling it now, if the information it contains was given or sold to certain other powers. We believe that all of these incidents are designed to embarrass the government by disrupting a major party conference and showing how easy it is to strike at the heart of democracy, and secondly, and more importantly to take our focus away from the theft of the flash drive, thus giving them time to reveal its contents while the conference is still going. So, three things! We find and incarcerate Reggie Parkes; we wipe out his terrorist network, and we retrieve the stick and return it to London. Easy!"

"Oh, and by the way, that information is to be kept Top Secret. In other words, you tell no one unless they have a need to know. Got It?"

Chapter Twenty Three

Reggie's mum and the SAS did not get on well with each other at first. Strangely enough, observed one of the soldiers, she didn't seem to mind that she had been abducted and put in a strange room, in a strange house, in a strange street. She actually seemed quite happy. But she wouldn't stop bloody talking.

The soldiers were polite when they spoke to her, which was sparingly, mainly because they couldn't get a word in edgeways, and while firm, they were surprisingly gentle in their manner and handling of her. Their own mums were like Reggie's mum and even those hard bitten SAS soldiers who would cut a throat on demand, anywhere in the world, in the most dire of circumstances on behalf of Her Majesty, were not about to deal roughly with someone who: a; was undoubtedly English; b; was elderly, c; could be their own mother, and d; was slightly batty and therefore vulnerable. Orders demanded however that she be kept safe and quiet until her son came to pick her up. This they would do, and then, they would deal with the son who was evidently a known, terrorist mastermind. That would be a different matter. It was not an easy task however, looking after the old bat. It soon became obvious that she had lost her marbles. Her ability to talk non-stop using what appeared to be hundreds of randomly generated words and statements, soon became more than irritating. It began to send them mad and they began to wonder if in fact she was completely insane and should be in a home, rather than being guarded by the SAS.

In short, it soon became obvious that not only was she was mad, but for some reason her madness demanded a computer, and until someone gave her one with a nice cup of tea, she would talk non-stop and even hinted at a bout of shrieking hysterics. Trooper C summed it up when he said to the boss that it was worse than the white noise he'd been subjected to whilst being held prisoner for training purposes in a heavily disguised barn not too far from Hereford. It was only when Trooper 'C', underestimating her ability with all things computer, and getting desperate, and with the permission of the boss, in writing, had given her one of their special, mobile un-hackable lightweight S4 super-notebooks, that she immediately quietened down. To their collective and enormous relief, Reggie's mum hunched over the little machine and lapsed into silence.

"Don't worry," said Trooper 'C' with a knowing wink to his compatriots. "She's a fruit cake, but that computer will keep her quiet for now. There're two games on it for her and I've shown her how to get into them." Solitaire and minesweeper were games deemed to provide SAS soldiers with lateral thinking training and so equipped all their notebooks. "Like a baby's toy," he added. "It's a backup anyway, so we don't need it unless one of the other ones blows up."

The unit was located in a small house in a temporary HQ in Westwood Avenue, taken over for the duration of the 'emergency' by a very reluctant Defence Secretary who only acceded to the request from the Home Secretary after pressure from the PM himself, in the name of a Mrs Mavis Axelrod and her four sons. Neighbours would later recall just how quiet and well behaved the new family were, as was proper in 'the Avenue'. The absence of a father to the family was explained by the fact that it was a military family, and he was most likely away serving Her Majesty. That explanation fully satisfied the Avenue.

But of course, like most things in Westbourne, it was not all as it seemed. Reggie's mum, though quiet, was in fact working hard. True, in her new role as keeper of the S4 super notebook, she talked to herself a lot, and Trooper 'C' was intrigued to hear her mumbling things like 'oh diligent software patching eh! They think they're good. Idiots! Anyone can get through that….oh, so that's what he's up to! I'd better tell Reggie about this.' But occasionally she would turn to Trooper 'C', grin, and talk gently about rockets, foreigners, strippers, whips and firewalls. She even rabbited on about chinchillas at one point. Mad as a hatter was the general verdict. But at least she was quiet now. And she couldn't communicate to anyone on that machine anyway. No way could she hack into the actual operating system! Not a mad old bat like her.

Outside the house in the Avenue, yellow lines kept the public from parking along most of the street, and these yellow lines, as is the nature of parking regulations were assiduously inspected by Traffic Wardens on a regular daily basis. Trooper 'C' had observed these regular patrols with amusement. "Fancy spending your life doing a job like that," he'd joked to his compatriots. 'Those Traffic Wardens! What a joke! Watching yellow lines all day. There aren't even any cars around to ticket! Pathetic! I'd like to see one of them in Sangin." If he had entered the presence of the patrols into his log, the very words 'Traffic Warden' would have lit up like a nuclear-powered beacon to certain of his superiors who were in the know, and subsequent events would perhaps have taken a very different course. But despite Trooper 'C's" high intelligence and carefully developed intuitive ability, honed on many extremely dangerous and complex operations, he didn't. To him, Traffic Wardens were like fleas and cockroaches. They existed. They were there. They were a normal feature of life. They were a pain in the arse. But they were no danger. Therefore, they didn't need to be mentioned in the log or considered.

To the rest of Westwood Avenue however, the presence of Traffic Wardens was a novelty and very welcome. The Avenue had long been one of those streets that were used as car parks by people heading into town for work either from the local rail station or by others who worked in the nearby business complex. They knew they were safe simply because everyone knew that Wardens visited this out of the way area only about once a year if that. By day four of the SAS occupancy of the Avenue however, the yellow lines were totally empty of cars; their owners now facing three days-worth of parking tickets.

Barbara had assigned Polly and Henrietta to observe the goings on in Westwood Avenue for the duration of what later became known in the town as 'the Westbourne terror', with strict instructions to keep an eye on number 72. "If they move, or if they go to the corner shop for anything, or even if the fart quietly, I want to know; OK?" There was no way either Polly or Henrietta would miss any of these simple indications. The landlord who lived next door at number 74 was Polly's father's ex third wife who had brought Polly up since she was 5, and the owner of the corner shop was Henrietta's daughter's Indian boyfriend's mother who used to be scared stiff of the word 'Police' on Henrietta's jumper in those days when they were Police Traffic Wardens. Police meant immigration, meant trouble, meant deportation, unless she behaved herself and did what Henrietta asked. The fact that Henrietta was now employed by the Council and was now officially called a Civil Enforcement Officer just made it worse. It was authority of the worst kind. What else did the word 'enforcement' mean? In her mind it meant double trouble.

"That's the advantage we have over those others, even the cops," Barbara had stressed to her troops. "It's our only advantage in fact, so we use it to the best. They have all of the sophisticated equipment, ninja fighters, listening posts, spooks, super computers and laser guns, hellfire missiles and so on, but we have contacts, and friends and people who owe us favours. And we know every inch of every street in this town. And that's what counts in this game. We're the locals. It's like them fighting Chechen guerrillas in Chechnya. You can't! Oh, and we also have Reggie's mum, who is now our super spy on the inside!"

The first fruit of Reggie's mum's labour came just a day and a half after her kidnapping when Keith received an encrypted message saying 'these boys make good tea. No rockets here, or whips or bad girls. Reggie can't afford to let me stay in this home? He's a good boy. Doesn't know anything about rockets. Bad pictures on this computer. Bad! Difficult computer.'

Keith ignored all the babble and swiftly downloaded the files attached to the message and gasped as he read a full set of instructions to the SAS unit passed down from London. He took the messages straight to Barbara.

Chapter Twenty Four

Barbara looked at the message with satisfaction and called a meeting of her special war cabinet which consisted of Dave, Dan, Jan, Reggie, Phyllis and Polly. Muggins stood guard at the door in his customary position, looking grimly at the door handle as though it was evil incarnate itself. Henrietta was deemed too dim to understand anything and anyway, she was likely to blab everything to someone like 'her Bill' with it all ending up in the press, so she was asked to keep watch at the front door of the station.

Barbara began, reading from the message passed to her by Reggie's mum. She read it carefully, not understanding everything, but enough to make plans.

"CRHI High Readiness State 2 Alert message: From Cabinet Office to Deployed Unit. Direct from PM. Obtain and retain package as necessary. Contact other party soonest and commence negotiations. Threats to other party. Use if required. High sanctions approved. Your discretion. Recovery of package a matter of national interest. Ack. Message ends"

"Looks good to me" exclaimed Barbara. They are beginning to panic nicely. We need to ramp up the pressure a bit so that there is even more panic. But we need to get to the PM and we never will unless he comes here. To this town."

A bit of disinformation is required as well, she thought. 'I'll speak to Dan about that, she mumbled quietly.'

"Now they want information about the package. They've instructed the boys in number 72 to contact Reggie. OK! They want information? We'll give them information. But we'll pre-empt them with a message of our own. No point in letting them in first. But we've got to make it sound good. No messing around. Jan, go tell Henrietta to get hold of Boobs. He might have been brought up in Cardiff's Tiger Bay, but he's of Arab descent via his grandfather, and he's a thespian. And now, he's about to play a starring part in this little drama - as an oriental terrorist! Tell her to take the van…. No, best forget that. Tell her to get a bus to his place."

It was just the evening before, when Barbara instructed Reggie to call the Police 0800 confidential, public information line. Phyllis had stood next to him as he carefully put a handkerchief over the mouthpiece and a peg on his nose. Reggie was nervous, which made the situation better because hopefully his voice would appear strained and edgy, just as it should be in the circumstances.

"We want to talk. The package for one million pounds and mum or we go to the press. Call this number by 8 am tomorrow. You'll know what I mean." He broke off, not knowing what more to say. Phyllis grinned at him and gave him the thumbs up.

The man on duty on the 0800 number was not in the employ of the police, and the number wasn't even in the police station. The call was answered by Trooper B in 72 Western Avenue, who turned and gave a 'thumbs up' to his colleagues. "They've taken the bait. I think it was that bloke Reggie himself, but they'll be able to match his voice….. His cell wants to negotiate. I've got a number for them to ring. He sounds nervous. Must be missing his mummy; poor bastard!"

Reggie felt weak after giving his message. He wasn't an actor of any kind and having to give a staged message over the phone like that undid his nerves, or so he felt. Phyllis helped him to a chair and wiped the beads of sweat from his forehead.

"It's not so much mum I'm worried about Phyllis," said Reggie accepting a stiff, rather more than double scotch. "She's a tough old bat and more than a match for the SAS. In fact, they'll be phoning in a day or two begging me to take her back. Probably even offer me money. You know what she's like. It's Roxy I'm worried about. I mean, what's going to happen to her? She's a nice girl. Pure. Those photos you mentioned must be spoofs. You know that. Someone told me what they can do on a computer nowadays. Airbrushes and all sorts of things."

He lapsed gloomily into silence vaguely wondering what an airbrush was.

Phyllis said nothing to that. She knew that Reggie doted on his niece and she knew that Roxy had a huge soft spot for Reggie, her favourite uncle. But she was a stunningly pretty girl, gregarious, and fun to be with, and a magnet for men. She didn't have much of an education; she had no trade, but she did have a body to die for and a face that would launch a bloody site more than a thousand ships. And anyway, from what she had heard on the grapevine, Roxy was having a ball, making money and enjoying every minute of it. Phyllis felt a momentary pang of envy. In fact a bit longer than momentary! Mind you she thought ruefully, even when she was young, she wouldn't have been of any interest whatsoever to men of power. She knew her own limitations in the looks department, but Reggie seemed to like her, and anyone who could care for his batty mother so well for so long and who believed in the purity of his niece was to her, a real man. Barbara had called Roxy, although she didn't know what had been said, but hoped Roxy was able to help. If it was to help her Uncle Reggie, then she would probably have agreed willingly. She was that type of girl.

Reggie had found where Roxy was staying and had told Barbara, but he didn't really think Roxy could help in any way. She wouldn't know anything. She was too nice and pure for all this sort of thing. He simply didn't understand anything about young, sexy good time girls and he didn't for a moment expect Roxy to be able to help. If there was anything in the business of Roxy and the Prime Minister that Phyllis had hinted at, it would be because although Roxy was a pure girl, she had somehow been ensnared against her will by powerful men in positions of authority, and her purity of spirit had been no armour in her protection. She was a helpless waif in a sea of corruption, sex, lies and probably drugs for all he knew. Anyone who looked as beautiful as her and as loving as her, couldn't possibly be doing any wrong.

"Bastards", he mouthed out loud as he sipped his scotch. He looked reflectively at the amber fluid and quietly resolved to sort matters out. "I'd better have another one of these Phyllis. Or maybe two!"

Back at number 72, Trooper B carefully encoded the recording as he'd been instructed, prepared the mega super top secret destination code and buzzed it in micro-milliseconds to control. He didn't know who control was, or where he was, and he didn't really care. All he knew was that he had to send to an encoded address and wait for an acknowledgement from a coded source. Mumbling wildly in the corner, Reggie's mum copied the code immediately and passed it on to her control, meaning Reggie and the gang in Barbara's office. She also picked up the encoded the acknowledgement and sent that on its way with the first message.

Having completer his task, Trooper B resumed his watch on the street, but saw nothing suspicious. Another two Traffic Wardens were walking by, though he couldn't imagine why as there were only two cars in the whole street. But there you go, he thought, people without brains are going to do things like that. One of them was a bit of a corker though, he had to admit. Nice legs and a fantastic arse, especially in that uniform. Time for a break though, he thought. He went and fetched Trooper D from the sitting room to take over the watch shift, and curled up in an armchair with the latest copy of Bee World; much more interesting than this particular job.

Reggie's mum recorded all the coded destinations, copied the decoding sequences, put down a marker to record and amend the daily code changes, advised all destinations about a new trip wire word which only she would know, organised block and auto-capture of all SAS burst transmissions, switched over to minesweeper, and gave Trooper D a half hour lecture on the importance of booster rockets in gaining escape velocity. After that, he left the room as fast as he could, and going to the window and pulling back the net, Reggie's mum signalled to Henrietta and Polly that all had been prepared. She was ready to transmit and receive and put into operation, Part One of the plan.

By seven thirty the next morning, quite a team had settled in a circle around Keith, in Barbara's sister's house. Reggie, Boobs, Phyllis, Barbara, Jan and Dave all stood in silence, looking serious and glancing expectantly at each other. Henrietta and Polly were still on watch in the vicinity of number 72. Muggins stood guard near the door, growling softly every now and again as if to reassure everyone that security was taken care of. Keith briefed Boobs for the tenth time that morning. Barbara knew that this message was all important. They needed panic and they needed the PM to visit Westbourne.

"When you answer the phone Boobs, don't go all squeaky as you have a habit of doing when your nerves play up. Keep it low, slow, calm and deadly serious. Use your Arab accent - you know the one you can do sometimes, it sounds foreign, and tell them straight. Tell them 'we are the cell members of the Heavenly Martyrs Brigade Southern England Branch Limited - got to make it sound legit; and we want money to help fund the continuing troubles in the lands of our righteous brothers across the seas. We also demand a statement from the cowardly Prime Minister who is sitting safe in London, away from the troubles of his people, oh and a statement condemning western aggression in various lands, and the withdrawal of every British soldier from the lands not British. Deliver the money to the following account number. Tell them when it is paid and when the Prime Minister makes his speech, here in this town otherwise he's a coward in the eyes of the world, we will give them further instructions. Say that if they fail us, we will blow up a strategic target and spread certain pictures and files over the web. Snowden is nothing on this. Or that other bloke. Can't remember his name. Barbara? The one stuck in that foreign embassy. No, don't say that Boobs. Just make something up. OK. But be firm and unpleasant. We need the PM here."

Boobs nodded He was pleased to be doing something for the group, but as secretary of the local cricket team, his nerves told him that he'd rather be at the cricket match he was meant to be playing in than performing in front of this serious group of Traffic Wardens. In fact, he was feeling more nervous than on a first night in the local theatre. He looked at Keith with a vaguely blank expression on his face.

"Shall I write it down Boobs?" asked Keith, alarmed.

"No, No! No No! No No No. Never!" Boobs shook his head violently. It would look unprofessional if he had to read lines, he thought. "I'll be fine Keith. Just let me …………" At that moment everyone jumped as the small mobile phone on the table suddenly rang. Boobs turning white, looked at it in horror, and then grimacing oddly, he picked it up, his hand shaking and said. "Can I help you boyo?"

"Arab, Boobs," whispered Keith savagely, "not bloody Welsh. You're a sodding foreigner."

Boobs looked at him aghast, nodded and plunged on. "We're martyrs in Southern England, not bloody Wales," he shouted down the phone. Then stopped and looked round wildly, already having forgotten his lines in his panic. "Give us the money or we'll blow up boyo. And we'll blow up in England as well and give the photos to the press and you'd better play cricket with us and that Prime Minister. He's a pervert bastard and had better make the speech, you dirty sssssssods…."

He started stuttering, something which he was also prone to whenever things got too much for him. It was the main reason he was always picked for silent parts in the local theatre productions. He had twice played a passer-by, a cleaner, a blind, deaf and dumb man, and a bit part as the back end of a camel in the Christmas story. He was only persuaded to do this when told that the front end didn't have a speaking part either. The front end did fart though, loudly and frequently, claiming that it added to the authenticity of the camel's persona, but nearly causing the collapse of Boobs due to the smell and the lack of oxygen. True, he had built up these small triumphs into something much larger when regaling his colleagues and friends in the Traffic Warden Service with his acting stories, but most people did that. Beads of sweat appeared on his brow and his hands shook more and more. Keith put his head in his hands.

Boobs plunged on desperately. "Oh yes, hold on boyo. The Prime Minister is a coward bastard, up in London when people here are suffering boyo! Sorry - I'm an Arab! Definitely not Welsh man. No, no, not Welsh. Oh! And another thing! Oh! Wwwwait a mmmmminute."

He covered the mouthpiece of the little phone and looked at Keith. "Kkkkeith boyo, what was that lllllast bit about…….".

Get him off the fucking phone," whispered Barbara savagely. Keith leapt up and grabbed the phone and in the ensuing scuffle, dropped it on the tiled floor, where it broke into what looked like million bits.

The group stood there looking at the pieces in horror. Keith broke the silence.

"Well, that's fucking that then isn't it! Well done Boobs, you've really…….."

He looked round at Boobs, but Boobs had already fled to the bathroom and could be heard gasping and retching into the toilet bowl. "Ah well," he said wearily, "at least Reggie's mum can filter it out and block it until we have another go. We'll have to get another phone. Probably best anyway for security. We can get a cheapie."

At the other end of the line, Trooper D listened in astonishment to what appeared to him to be some sort of

Welshman threatening to blow up the English and a load of other gibberish that he couldn't quite grasp. He looked at Trooper C and his boss, who both looked just as baffled as he did. "Seems like Welsh Nationalists have joined the cause now. Did you get any of that lads?" None of the troopers had understood much at all. "Oh well" grinned the boss, we'll just send it by burst to Control and see what happens. No need for us to understand it. They've got experts to decipher crap like that." He grinned. "Bloody funny accent that guy had. Couldn't work out whether it was Welsh, Geordie, Dutch or what. Didn't sound much like an Arab anyway." He shrugged and ordered Trooper D to transmit.

Reggie's mum had understood Boob's message perfectly. It was all crystal clear to her. Her team wanted money and they would blow themselves up if they didn't get it. And the Prime Minister was a perv. Well she didn't know that before, but obviously Reggie's team knew best and if they said the PM was a perv, then he was. And they would show the photos as well. Rockets she thought. Perfectly obvious and a very sensible approach. All clear as crystal. She would allow the message to be sent to Control. It seemed that the SAS troopers had grasped the essentials. They were grinning. Keith had told her to intercept and block it if it had gone wrong, or if Boobs had screwed up, but as it made eminent good sense, she removed the block and Trooper C sent the message to his control, which she'd traced to the Cabinet Office whatever that was. Probably some cupboard they kept the cups and saucers in up in London or somewhere. She'd have to ask Reggie about that if she could remember it.

Boobs reappeared in the room looking pale and anxious. "How did I do Keith?" He asked worriedly. Not liking the look Keith gave him, he appealed to Barbara. "Barbara?" He looked around. "Guys?" No one spoke and he gave up and sat down miserably.

Barbara went over to the cupboard and retrieved a large bottle of scotch and six tea cups. Sod the piles she thought, and sod the herpes. I'm going to need this. Although Reggie's mum could be relied on to prevent that farcical speech from Boobs getting through, she asked Keith to send her a quick message to remind her that at all costs it should be stopped. But just as she spoke, the computer screen lit up as Reggie's mum's message came through. She brightened. Salvation she thought. At least we get another chance. She'll have blocked that gibberish. Well done Reggie's mum, she thought. She looked at the screen.

Good message. Crystal clear! Sent to Control by troopers. Troopers liked it. Boobs is a good boy. Does a really good message. Are the Welsh joining in? Good team. Message forwarded. No worries. All done.

Barbara poured the scotches and sat down. She realised then that she hadn't thought through the bit about involving Reggie's mum at all well. This could cost them dear.

Chapter Twenty Five

"Where are you heading off to Dan?" Dave called from the steps of the Police station.

"Got an appointment," mumbled Dan. "With the nurse. She's visiting today. Having a wart frozen off." He brushed passed Dave without really facing him or looking at him in the eye, and headed off up the vestibule stairs.

"Odd!" muttered Dave quietly. 'Dan never mentioned he had warts.' But he needed to get to Barbara's office quickly, so he moved on without further comment. The team had been called in early. There had been developments on the message that Reggie's mum had passed on last night. She'd sent a new message this morning. Shame Dan can't be there he thought, as he entered the office and saw the rest of the team sitting round the table.

"Dan's gone to see the nurse, Barbara................"

"Never mind about that Dave", called Barbara. "We've got other things to think about now. The shit's hit the fan. And remarkably, it's in our favour. Our shit deflectors worked for once. There's probably no need to get another cell phone. Reggie's mum has passed us this message." She handed the piece of paper to Dave, who read it quickly, his eyes widening. He read it out loud.

'*For squad Alpha*'. "*Threat level lifted to imminent attack, Code RED. Threat more serious. Vulture will visit town to show solidarity. Highest security. Programme follows. Further: Probability of coordinated attacks in city centres using suicide bombers. Welsh and English cities likely targets. Tasks now: Find the Traffic Warden. Use any, repeat any tactics necessary. Any negotiation. Package must be retrieved at all costs. Vulture and Goshawk coming to your operations centre. ETA 1400 hrs Local for update.*"

"Slippery Liz told us in the meeting yesterday that Vulture and Goshawk are the PM and the Home Secretary, and they're coming here," added Barbara with satisfaction. "They were worried about a message received yesterday. It seemed to call the PM a coward. Anyway, because of it, he and the Home Secretary are coming to Westbourne to 'cheer us up' and 'show solidarity'. So well done to Boobs. Now we can sort this thing out." She looked round. "Now, he'll be staying at the Grand of course, but we know from Roxy that he'll be with her at the Old Manse from about midnight to seven in the morning. You know, the big old house just out of town. Only one chauffer bodyguard and two gate guards will be with him so as to keep it discreet, and according to Roxy, only we know this so, it's highly secret. I advised Liz that it might be a good idea for me to pay a visit and brief him on the situation at the hotel, except it won't be at the hotel. Why me? Why not the Chief Constable herself? Because we won't be noticed. We don't attract attention. We won't drag the hordes of press with us. We're what you'd call discreet. And anyway, Liz wants to keep an overall eye on things from Police HQ. She told us to call by at 5.30 in the morning. The PM has an early start and I can brief him before he leaves. Jan, Dan, Polly, Henrietta and Dave will all come with me in the cone van to the Manse that morning. Reggie, call Roxy and let her know. Keith, you go and buy the fireworks. Liz will let the PM's staff know we're coming."

Dan left Dibsey's office furtively. He looked up and down the corridor and only when he decided it was safe, did he emerge and walk towards the corridor exit door and onwards to the Chief Superintendent's office. His mission had been simple, and Dibsey had been keen to encourage him. It had gone well.

"So what do you want Mr   er…"

"Dan" replied Dan nervously. My name's Dan."

"Well, Dan, what seems to be the trouble? Or if there's no trouble, how can I help you?"

"I know where Reggie is."

"And just where is he and why are you telling me?"

"I'm pissed off with all this terrorism thing and because of it all, they've taken my van away. I loved driving that cone van, and now someone who's actually crashed it is still driving it. She doesn't know anything about van driving. All she is, is a speed merchant. Merchant of death more like. Silly cow!" He spat contemptuously.

Dibsey wasn't too sure which particular silly cow, Dan was referring to among many in the Traffic Warden crew, but he was eager to hear what Dan had to say about Reggie. This could be his big break. If he could sort out this bastard, the whole terrorism thing would come to an end. If he played his cards right. And that meant not saying a dicky bird to Liz, Monty, or anyone else. Except of course the SAS.

"Well where is he?"

"Who'll know I said?" said Dan belligerently. He didn't like Dibsey at the best of times, and he didn't trust him not to tell the rest of the Wardens that he'd blabbed.

"Me and me only, I can assure you of that Mr Traffic Warden. OK?" Dibsey had no intention whatever of sharing this gem with anyone except the SAS boss, and then only because he needed them. His confidence in organising his own show had evaporated after the Shelley mansions fiasco. Better leave it to the experts this time.

"OK" said Dan, "but if you breathe a word Inspector, I'll 'ave you. Got it?"

Dibsey flinched, but nodded his head. He'd sort the Warden out at a later date. No one threatens the

Police, especially not a poxy, low-life Traffic Warden. 'Later my boy', he thought maliciously.

"Well, he's staying with his niece, Roxy in the Old Manse on the Welford Road. You'll know the place. Belongs to a city gent, but he lets it out. It's his niece that's got the package you lot have been looking for. I heard 'im say it. And she ain't about to give it up, until her uncle Reggie says so."

"Are you certain of this, because……"

"Totally certain, but you don't have to believe me. I can take my information elsewhere. Your Chief Super would like to know…."

"OK, OK, OK. I believe you. Will he be there all day?"

"I don't know his movements. You can get that from your own bosses."

"Well, many thanks, Dan, is it? Yes, many thanks Dan, and not a word to anyone else, OK? Wouldn't want an operation of this importance to fail because of a slipped word would we. So off you go then, and I'll be in touch."

'Prick' thought Dan as he left. As for not saying anything to anyone else, well he had another office to visit, and a phone call to make. He wanted to ensure his message got round.

When the phone rang in Brigadier Archie Paine's office, he nearly didn't pick it up. His world was falling apart, what with one thing and another, and the fiasco down in Westbourne left him feeling sick. How the hell had that happened? More Juju! His own men fighting the police and managing to destroy the house and any evidence that it may have held. He looked at the phone maliciously and grabbed it to his mouth.

"Fitzpaine here, " he barked.

"Dan here" came the reply. In Archie's line of work, such a phone call was all part of the business. He didn't know who Dan was and he didn't care. Whether he kept the phone in his hand or not depended on what this Dan fellow had to say.

"Well Dan, whoever you are, what have you to say?"

"Reggie Parkes will be in the Old Manse on the Welford Road out of Westbourne overnight. He moves around a lot, but he'll be there at around 5.30 onwards in the morning."

"How do I know that's the truth?"

"Do you want the package or not?" The phone went dead.

Archie dialled a number. "Red Four? You'll have orders within the hour. Be ready to move. And this time, no fuck ups. Got it?"

Over in their hidden and highly secret location, Trooper D and his boss also looked at the signal from

Control, but for them, it was a cause of great alarm. It meant a personal visit by VIPs, and that was never a good thing, personally or operationally.

"I told you they'd be able to understand it better than us boss. Bit of a bastard them coming down here though. The PM and the Home Secretary. We'd better tidy up a bit."

They both jumped as the phone rang. Trooper C who had woken up and come into the ops room answered it sleepily. He listened for a small while and handed it to the boss. "It's for you, boss. An Inspector Dibswell of the Police."

"Inspector, how can I help?" He wondered how the Police not only knew who he was but where he was. But there we are he thought, tell a secret to more than one person and it's no longer a secret.

"Detective Inspector please. Anyway, I know how to find Reggie."

Silence for five seconds.

"How Detective Inspector?" The boss wasn't a man of many words, if just three would do.

He listened as Dibsey explained his plan.

"So we'll be in place at seven tomorrow morning then."

"On the dot please."

The boss put his phone down, shouted at Trooper D to go and try and shut that bloody woman up, and called his team together. It looked as though the whole thing might be easier than he thought, and the added bonus was that they could get rid of Reggie's mum at last. She was beginning to test even his famous calm. They should use the old bat as a weapon against the Russian spetznatz.

"Oh, and by the way, we'll be there at six."

Barbara in the meantime, read the message that came through from Reggie's mum and smiled. It seemed that matters were going her way. The message simply said. "All good here."

She had gathered her crisis team together after the morning brief and set out her plans for the day. Dan was looking a bit grumpy, and everyone supposed it was because she'd kept him off van driving. But he was a big boy now and should be able to take the rough with the smooth. In reality it was because his feet were becoming increasingly sore and uncomfortable. Reggie sat there looking worried and Phyllis held her arm round him as though to comfort him.

"OK everyone. Listen in. Reggie, you're going to stay at my sister's place tonight and tomorrow. We want you out of the way. Now don't worry, no-one will know where you are until they need to. We've all kept her place a huge secret. I'll brief you more fully later, on the way there. Oh! And Keith, give that reporter woman a ring will you. You know the one, that Johnson woman. She always appears to be ahead of the game somehow. I need to talk to her. They want terrorists, we'll give them terrorists. And they can all fight amongst themselves, as long as we get the PM on his own."

Barbara looked round menacingly, mentally warning everyone that secrets were secrets and never to be passed on, and continued on to explain the rest of the day's news. The papers knew about it anyway and blazoned it in headlines, led of course by the indomitable Jennifer Johnson.

"Prime Minister to visit brave siege town"
Exclusive story from Jennifer Johnson, Political Editor

The Prime Minister and the Home Secretary are to make a short visit to Westbourne tomorrow at around lunch time. The PM's staff told me that the reason for the visit was to discuss the unfolding terror situation with the Civil Power in the county, and for the PM to see for himself how the military forces were successfully aiding that power. He also wants to show solidarity with the people of the County who have suffered so much turmoil.

The Cabinet Office have given advance notice of the visit in spite of the security risk as they believe that the Government should be as much involved as possible with the people at this time of trial. The Prime Minister will arrive ahead of the Home Secretary to complete other business before making a speech at City Hall where it is believed he will again stress his opposition to the terrorist aims and thank the police and other services for their professionalism. Security is expected to be tight. We will report more on the developing story throughout the morning.

Excellent thought Barbara. And he will no doubt be staying with Roxy while he 'completes his other business', and with him and her well ensconced in the Old Manse on the Welford Road, her plan could even work. There'd be risk involved, and they'd all get the sack if it went wrong. But what the hell, she was going to retire soon anyway.

Chapter Twenty Six

Barbara ran over the plan in her mind for the fiftieth time as she sat at home sipping another scotch. It would be an early start for all of them, she knew, but by lunchtime, it would all be over, one way or another. She would either be retiring with an honourable pension, or be sacked and get nothing. 'Everything to play for then,' she thought, and poured another generous measure. 'I've briefed everyone and now it's up to them' she thought as she changed for bed. Her last thoughts as she drifted into sleep centred on Reggie. Reggie the hero? Or Reggie the idiot? She could never make up her mind. It was an awful night. One of those in which you never really knew whether you were sleeping or not, and whether asleep or awake, everything seemed weird. She woke to the alarm at four thirty and blearily dressed and made a cup of tea. She couldn't face any food. Too nervous, too early, and too shit scared. All they had to do was provide a terrorist raid, somehow extract the PM, and convince various authorities that everything was in order.

The cone van arrived at five. It was cold but bright and the van contained Keith, Dave, Polly, Henrietta and twenty five cones just in case. Neither Jan nor Dan would dare omit cones from any task. You just never knew when they'd come in handy.

"OK everyone," said Barbara blearily, "let's do this. No fuck ups. Jan if you crash this bloody thing, before we're done, I'll kill you again. I'll actually be with you this time, so I'll make sure of the job."

Jan drove off unsteadily and whispered to Dave, "I hate being under the spotlight like this. The pressure gets to me. You heard what she said." She looked intently through the windscreen, blinking rapidly. Dave squeezed her hand gently on the wheel. Jan smiled and her nerve steadied. Fifteen minutes later the van drew up at the gates to the Old Manse and Jan stared into the face of a particularly tough and mean looking, well-dressed man. He had an earpiece and one of those coiled leads coming out of his ear.

"Yes?"

"We're here to see Goshawk."

Jan waited until the man had finished mumbling into his lapel mike. He then ordered everyone out and while his companion watched over them shivering on the verge, thug features inspected the inside and underneath of the van. He finally got up and came over to them.

"Passes," he barked. They all held out their Traffic Warden passes and he consulted a list of names and photos and then stared at them all in turn.

Barbara began to get worried. 'This is taking far too long. Other things would happen if they didn't get a move on quickly.' She looked at her watch. "Shit almost six. For fuck's sake hurry up man," she said under her breath.

"OK. Pass through". They clambered back into the van as the gates opened and the cone van swept through and up the drive to the old house. Two minutes later Barbara was in the presence of the Prime Minister and his bodyguard. Roxy was nowhere to be seen. Jan and Dave stayed in the van outside in case of the need for an urgent getaway. Keith, Polly and Henrietta went down to the kitchens, carrying a large box.

"OK," said Keith quietly, let's get these boxes of bangers out the back door and set them off in the yard." He carried the first two of three large boxes stuffed with fireworks and placed it outside the house near to the grand sitting room. "Think I might have overdone it here with these fireworks," he muttered. "Mind you, might as well make sure the PM hears the bangers when they go off. Waste of time otherwise. Now who's got the matches?"

Polly and Henrietta looked blankly at each other and then equally blankly at Keith. Henrietta's mouth began to droop and tears sprouted from her eyes.

"Oh Keith, no one said anything about matches."

"Well how the bloody hell do you think we light these things then? OK, OK, don't start bawling for heaven's sake. None of us thought of the bloody things. Quick, go and have a look in the kitchen." He sat down wearily as the girls shot into the kitchen to start their search. 'I'm not sure I can go on like this' he thought.

It seemed like hours before Polly rushed out of the kitchen with one of those gas lighter things that many gas kitchens use. 'Thank God for that,' thought Keith." He pulled the trigger and nothing happened. Polly and Henrietta looked on in anguish. "No sodding gas. Look, get in that kitchen and light a bit of newspaper or something from the gas cooker. Hurry! Barbara will be getting frantic."

They shot back into the kitchen and Polly rolled up some newspaper and held it over the gas flame on one of the rings that thankfully fired up immediately on a clicker. They rushed outside.

"Here you go Keith." The flames from the piece of newspaper had started to lick up around her hand and she bumped into Henrietta in her haste to pass the burning roll to Keith, tripped over the first box and dropped the burning roll directly into the second firework box. Several fuses started fizzing immediately and they all looked at it in horrified silence for a couple of seconds before Keith shouted "Run. Fucking run!"

In the sitting room of the Old Manse, the Prime Minister's face was wreathed in smiles. He'd had a jolly time overnight with Roxy and was looking forward to a hearty breakfast before beginning the travails of the day. He stood up as Barbara entered the room.

"Barbara, isn't it?" He said cordially. "Well, according to my notes from the Chief Constable you are. Take a seat. Please. I understand you're here to brief me on the situation in town from which I hear the Traffic Warden force has played an outstanding part if I may say. Well done." He smiled again and sat back in his armchair.

Barbara felt herself warming to this man. He might play around with teenies, albeit just old enough, but he was a charmer, and quite good looking in the flesh.

"That's right Prime Minister. The Chief felt it best to keep it all low key and of course discreet. She gave the PM a knowing smile, and glanced up the stairs.

"Yes, yes, quite so," he agreed.

Barbara continued. "If she had swept in here, just about everyone else would have as well. Reporters; the lot. They always seem to know where she is. No one takes much notice of us though. And anyway, with all the commotion going on she's sitting in the Police control centre keeping a close eye on the situation. But let me start on the briefing. Er, well as you know we find ourselves in an awkward situation……" Where the hell was Keith and the fireworks? She hadn't got anything to say and the bangs should have started by now. "Anyway, Prime Minister, you are well aware of the situation we er find ourselves in and well, er how we got here…." She felt herself beginning to babble and going red.

"Well yes Barbara, I have an overall picture, but what I want from you is the details. So far you haven't told me anything I don't already know. I mean what, for instance, is the status of our forces down here; are the police manning situation sufficient for the task, and what about......."

They both flinched and cowered as a huge explosion went off somewhere near the house and the sitting room windows shattered, spraying glass everywhere. Barbara was expecting some noise, but she thought a series of smallish bangs had been planned, not this. A second huge explosion and the sound of more glass shattering somewhere in the house preceded the sudden appearance of Polly and Henrietta into the sitting room followed by one of the PM's security detail. The PM looked at his man askance just as a rocket shot through the window and blew up with a bang and a shower of sparks on the far wall of the sitting room and set light to the art deco embroidered tasselled net chateaux curtains.

"Well!" he barked. "What the hell's going on man?" He glanced uneasily at the flames beginning to climb the walls."

"Not sure, sir. I've just been on to the SAS and they think it's a terrorist attack. They'll follow up this end, but we need to get you out of here."

Thank God for that thought Barbara. A bit more than I expected, but it seems to have worked. She looked at the PM. "Sir, we have a safe, fallback position at Police HQ in the town. We were fully briefed on it by the Chief Constable. We'll take you there now. Can we go in your car? Polly, get an extinguisher or this lot will go up."

The PM looked at Barbara as though deciding whether he could trust her or not, and then appeared to make up his mind. "OK, let's go now." He shouted over to his bodyguard. "Call in the men at the gate. We all go together."

They rushed out to the car and under Barbara's directions, set off towards town and Police headquarters. As they swept passed the cone van and out of the estate's back entrance, well away from any interference by others, Barbara gave Dave and Jan the nod. Polly and Henrietta followed them out having extinguished the flames quickly and efficiently.

"Polly, we'd better drag that big box inside. Barbara might need those fireworks again and what if it rains?" They dragged the box into the kitchen, sweating at its size and weight. "Must be a ton of the things," gasped Polly. "Ok, we'll leave them here in the kitchen. Come on, let's split." They raced out of the door and into the van.

Out on the Northern Perimeter of the Old Manse grounds, well hidden in a low hedge, the Boss looked in alarm at his men. "Looks like trouble lads. The effing terrorists are firing at someone or something. Let's move.

Take the house and get that bastard Reggie. I'm sick to death of him." The troops moved rapidly towards the Old Manse. Ready for anything.

At exactly the same time, Archie Fitzpaine let out a shout. He had decided to attend in person this time. No more fuck ups was his mantra for this operation. He needed that flash drive for the Home Secretary and in that house was the bastard terrorist who had it. Nothing would stop him this time.

"Move Move Move. Move on the house. C'mon Jamie! Get those men in." His men in black moved forward, and the first firing started.

Jan and Dave with Polly and Henrietta in the back, set off up the road after the PM's car, but at a more leisurely pace. At two crossroads they placed cones from the van across the roads effectively blocking them from all traffic. Strung between the cones, they ran Police no entry tape. With the whole county in an uproar over terrorism, no-one was going to pass these. Having covered their tracks with a few more road closures, they headed back to HQ in town, ready to assist the authorities in any way they could.

Chapter Twenty Seven

Chief Superintendent Monty Mathews had had a bad night. Like Barbara, his dreams were weird, but all centred on Traffic Warden weirdness. It just wouldn't go away. At five in the morning, he woke up with a start and shot upright in his bed, his brain working madly. "It's the bloody Traffic Wardens! They're behind all this. It's nothing to do with terrorists or any of that shit!"

Monty drew in his breath noisily as he realised the true import of his deliberations. He had sat up half the night in his office poring over every report written on this terrorism threat to his town. He had looked at every angle and analysed every move made by the terrorists and the police. He had read every report in the papers written by that Jennifer Johnson woman. And he couldn't actually see anything too out of the ordinary. True, there were a whole heap of isolated incidents; a robbery foiled by a Traffic Warden, a fire witnessed by Traffic Wardens, an explosion at a substation, witnessed by Traffic Wardens; three Traffic Warden cone van crashes, and a suspicious foreigner chased and caught by Traffic Wardens - and strangely released on orders from London. And true, he was under pressure from the Home Secretary to get hold of a stolen flash drive held by a hero Traffic Warden supposedly turned terrorist. But there was no real substance to any of it that would suggest terrorism. No-one had been killed. No hideous deaths to report in the papers. Yet here they all were. A whole town virtually under martial law. Troops and armed police all over the place. Aircraft and warships. Speeches in the House. But nothing really had happened, unless the Traffic Wardens were involved, and even then, nothing major.

Monty stood up in his pyjamas and gazed out of the window pensively. All along he had thought something odd about this terrorist business. Even the crashes of police vans were Traffic Wardens, One of them into a pub. Right into it. The bloody van ended up at the bar! Doing what though he wondered? What the hell were they up to? After a millisecond of further reflection, he decided it didn't matter. He'd have the whole lot banged up. Precautionary measures. Easy to implement in times like this. Terrorism and all that, even though he was convinced there wasn't any. And he had the authority to do it, even without permission from Slippery Liz. She was Chief Constable. County. But Westbourne was his. He could usually rely on a good sleep to bring out the right solutions. Why hadn't he thought of it all before, he asked himself angrily?

He picked up the phone and told the night watch to get hold of Detective Inspector Dibswell immediately. "Yes, now! Right now! I don't care where he is, or what he's doing. Even if he's at a bloody funeral, drag him out and get him on the phone." He'd have them all in cells within a couple of hours and then he'd find out exactly what was going on. Within five minutes, a worried Dibsey called his chief and was told to get a squad of as many men as possible, including the twenty on call armed men to the Old Manse as soon as possible. It was five thirty now. They should be able to get there by six.

"What? Right now Sir?"

Yes Chief inspector. Right bloody now! Just do it. I don't know what the bastards are up to but whatever it is we've got to stop them before something else goes up in smoke."

His red phone went off and he grabbed it in irritation. "What?"

He listened in amazement at what was going on. The Old Manse was under attack by terrorists. A Traffic Warden van had passed through the gate fifteen minutes beforehand. The whereabouts of the PM was unknown. Assumed in the Grand with his local tart.

"I knew it," he exclaimed out loud. Traffic Wardens again. I'll have those bastards. He picked up his phone again. "Chief Inspector. Forget the Old Manse. Get everyone you can to HQ. NOW! I'll see you there. And don't go anywhere until I get there. Oh, and send a man round to the Grand to see if the PM is there still."

"But Sir. I'm hearing over the net that everything's happening at the Old Manse, shouldn't we go there?"

"No. NO! Definitely not! That's just where those bloody Traffic Wardens want us to go. It's a decoy. The PM won't be there. Get everyone to HQ and we'll sort it out from here. Now Inspector! Bloody now!"

By the time Monty had dressed and raced down the stairs to his car, Dibsey was on the phone again.

"The Old Manse is under attack sir. Just heard from the SAS. Sir, I've diverted our men to that location. I had to. Slippery… sorry, I mean the Chief Constable has ordered it. You'd better get there too sir. I'll see you there." He clicked off.

Monty groaned. It would be the Traffic Wardens. He knew that. How they had pulled off a fake attack and for what reason, he didn't know, but it would be them without any doubt. He'd go there and say I told you so, but whatever they were up to, he'd ensure they didn't get away with it this time.

Chapter Twenty Eight

"Right" shouted Monty as he got out of his car at the old Manse. "As we're wasting our time here, we might as well nab those bloody wardens, because that's who it'll be. We move up to the house. We surround it and we arrest at gunpoint anyone coming out of it. Keep the dogs ready to tear any of the sods limb from limb if they so much as blink nastily at you. And don't worry. They'll all be Traffic Wardens alright. There'll be no problems with them."

Monty was pleased that he'd brought the armed offenders squad. Twenty good men, backed up with another forty brought along by Chief Inspector Dibswell. And the dogs. He knew there would be no trouble with these cretins, but having armed men around was comforting. And the dogs always scared the shit out of even hardened criminals let alone effing wardens. He couldn't wait. And anyway, just in case there was something in all this, the armed men would sort it out. The men filed obediently through the gate at his command and moved quietly into position around the house.

Archie's men, with Archie himself at their head moved into the rear door of the Old Manse. There was to be no possibility of recognition this time and so rough dress was the order of the day. Jeans, T shirts, bovver boots and well blacked up. They might have looked like ruffians but their professionalism was undiminished. They were silent and they were efficient. They didn't train with the SAS for nothing. Two explosions had occurred and the rear of the house was a mess. The men moved carefully. Ready for anything.

"There's movement in there sir," one of the men muttered. "Near the front of the house. Probably the terrorists." They crouched down as one and started to make their way forward through the rooms.

"Here! We stop here until we can locate the bastards," whispered Archie. He waved his arm down and the men crouched again. "Keep your fire. Hold still until we find out more. If anyone comes in throw stun grenades. Just be prepared for the noise OK?" They were in the beautiful Georgian sitting room, amply provided with cover from solid armchairs and sofas. They waited. Ready.

The Boss moved ahead of his men in a direct frontal assault on the front of the Old Manse. He had briefed them well. "If they're in there we'll have them. Straight in, no messing. Usual search pattern. Total silence. Arrest or kill, but keep that bastard Parkes alive and well. Got it?" The men nodded and moved on the house. They flowed in through the front door, crouching down and keeping their weapons trained on the doors and openings in front of them.

"There's movement in that far room Boss" whispered the Sergeant. He held out his hand to slow the squad down.

"OK. Simple. No point in pissing around, they're only terrorists. We go in NOW! GO!"

They smashed the sitting room door down, threw four stun grenades in, and the world blew up in front of them.

The small spark that had fizzed away in the large firework box since the first explosion met with the blue touch paper of a large banger. The blue touch paper smoldered away for a short while and the large banger blew up and set fire to the box itself. Two seconds later, the box blew up. The devastation was truly startling. Windows, half a wall into the sitting room, most of a ceiling. All gone in seconds. This explosion plus the stun grenade explosions was too much for all involved. The curtains were well and truly on fire and it was spreading merrily in all directions. Dazed and bleeding men, some carrying others staggered out of the house into the waiting arms, and guns of Monty's waiting men who swiftly and efficiently disarmed any still carrying and sat them down on the ground with their hands cuffed behind their backs. Monty looked at them dispassionately.

"Better phone for the ambulance and the fire brigade Chief Inspector, and send a couple of Police medics in to make sure there are no bodies or injured. Quick man before those flames take hold. Then bring the transports up and we'll take these bastards to the cells." Dibsey looked at him in amazement and ordered one of his men to make the calls. "Oh, and tell the Chief. She'll be at HQ. Let her know what's what." He looked at the men sitting and lying on the ground. He was beginning to have a horrible suspicion that they were not Traffic Wardens. And if they weren't, he thought, who the fucking hell were they?

The ambulances arrived first, followed a minute later by the first two fire engines. For a while, efficiency reigned supreme.

"Oh God" exclaimed the first paramedic to alight from an ambulance. It's this bloody lot again. And I thought I saw that reporter woman on the drive as we came in. Well, they'd better bloody well behave this time."

The injured were dealt with swiftly and efficiently. No one was too badly hurt and they were soon loaded up into the ambulances. Dibsey ordered two policemen into each ambulance to keep an eye on the prisoners and as a 'just in case' policy. Any of those bastards could be faking it he thought. None of them were that badly injured. More dazed than anything. "You stay in hospital with them. You don't let them out of your sight."

"Well that's all the injured sorted Chief Superintendent," reported the Chief ambulance officer. We'll be off. The fire chief has told me there's no-one left inside the house, but he doesn't reckon they'll save the house. Too much wood in these old places. Very flammable. Difficult to control."

Monty nodded. There were five engines now trying to fight the fire and it didn't seem to be going well. He flinched as the whole West wing of the house collapsed in a massive shower of bangs and sparks.

"Oh well, come on Brightwell. Let's get back to base. Nothing more we can do here. Those buggers have done it again somehow. We'll go and report to Liz and then see to those bastards in the cells."

Jennifer Johnson smiled happily as she approached the two policemen. She had captured everything on film from start to finish, thanks to an anonymous tip off from some Scottish sounding woman yesterday who had flattered her on her accurate and informative reports. She had arrived early enough to witness armed men approaching the house, and had witnessed what appeared to be an attack on the location of terrorist in chief, Reggie himself. Wonderful!

"Oh Inspector, do you have any words for the press about this evening's events?"

"Foxtrot Oscar:" scowled Dibsey as he headed for his car.

"I beg your pardon Inspector."

"Fuck Off" he replied. "And it's fucking Detective Inspector. Got it? Now write that down you cretin." He slammed his car door.

Rude man, she thought, I bet there's no such rank. Fucking Detective Inspector? What sort of rank is that with a swear word in it? But really, she wasn't dissatisfied with his response. It would all be reported whether he spoke or not. By being rude to her he had just effectively given her licence to report what she interpreted the events to be. She'd worked that out in her mind ages ago as a very junior cub reporter just a couple of weeks ago. Well, it seemed like ages. Really, she had only been a reporter for three months. But she had had several promotions already and she was enjoying herself immensely. She looked back at the burning house and wondered thoughtfully back to her car, already creating the new headlines in her mind.

Chapter Twenty Nine

As Barbara talked to the Prime Minister, they rode smoothly along the Westbourne expressway in the very nice PM's car, followed by the two gate men in another equally impressive car and by the time they reached Westbourne, the PM had been convinced of the truth of the matter. An attempt on his life. The explosions at the Old Manse, clear evidence of an assassination attempt in his view, had shaken him to the core. He realized what a fool he'd been putting himself in such danger while there were terrorists overrunning the County. And he had felt so vulnerable. Thank God for the Traffic Wardens, people he'd always instinctively disliked before. Mind you, anyone who could drive a Police van right up to a bar of a pub obviously had some sort of spark in them.

He had gradually relaxed in the comfort of the car and Barbara briefed him on the whole story from the time Reggie interrupted the robbers to the explosions at the Old Manse a few minutes ago, including Roxy's part in it and the fact that she was Reggie's adored niece. The PM sat back in shock, while his over activated mind took it all in.

"So what we have," exclaimed the Prime Minister in amazement is a potential attempted blackmail of me with some dubious pictures, by a person or persons unknown - a bit embarrassing I might say Barbara." He winked at her and her heart fluttered again. He continued.

"And a contract signed by me apparently, to sell modern British weapons to one of the worst and most repressive regimes in the world, and an entire anti-terrorism operation involving thousands of people and millions of pounds to counter a problem that actually didn't exist. The terrorists are all members of the security forces of one stripe or another, even that foreign guy apparently. My God, a whole county mobilised over nothing. Even a bloody AWACs from the RAF! Do you know how much an hour it costs to fly one of those things? And a billion pound warship sitting idly off the coast! You realise what would happen if this got out; the government could fall. Of shear ridicule if nothing else. Not to mention the total failure of the intelligence services, the Home Office, the SAS and of course the vast amount of wasted money involved." He sat back in the chair, a stunned look on his face.

"Exactly Prime Minister, " said Barbara, pleased that this pleasant and rather good looking man had grasped the essentials so quickly. She could easily see how young ladies could have a good time with him, but she desisted from asking him about the balloons in the photo.

"But this flash drive?" he had asked in true amazement when Barbara had first mentioned it. "I don't know anything about a flash drive." He looked round as though someone would burst in at any moment and blow him up again.

"But someone did Prime Minister," replied Barbara, and I have a hunch about that. She then told the Prime Minister about the very first people who came down from London to 'interview' Reggie, and how a Mr Percy Smythe, with an 'e' had linked Reggie's name to terrorism and threatened him with all sorts of dire consequences if he failed to reveal the location of the package containing the flash drive. "That's when all this terrorism stuff started."

"The PM looked at his bodyguard. "Know him Bentley? This Smythe fellow"

"Know of him, sir. One of those arrogant sods from that MI5 offshoot. Can't remember what it's called. Does special jobs for the Home Secretary. Or for you if you wanted them to, but works directly under the Home Secretary. Think they were Gods to see them strutting around." He returned his gaze to the window and scanned the approaches to the house.

The PM looked at Barbara. "Well, Madam Traffic Warden? What do you think?"

"You see sir, I think someone was sending that drive to the Home Secretary. Someone who had coded it up and set all the protections on it. You know; protections from prying eyes. So that only he could get into it. Just in case it was stolen. Some computer whizz kid or other.

What he didn't reckon on was the strange but true genius of Traffic Warden Parkes's mum. She might be batty, but she does know her computers."

"But why by post?" asked the Prime Minister. "I mean there are loads of better ways; couriers and so on."

Barbara smiled. "The post is usually a very safe way of moving sensitive material about the world. There's so much of it, no-one usually takes any notice of it. That's why diamonds are often moved by letter sized packages in the regular post. Also, it's anonymous. No-one can trace a letter back to the sender unless they want it to be known who they are. Use couriers or registered post and you have to give names and details and all that type of thing. With this being so sensitive, it could be downright dangerous for the sender if he or she was found out. And by email, it could be hacked easily and if something gets on the net, it's there for all to see if they look."

The Prime Minister sat up straight. "So it could be the Home Secretary? He's the one who's using his men to reclaim the thing after all. And he has never told me about it. The bastard! But can we prove it Barbara? I'm not sure about that. He'll just deny it."

Well, there's one way to settle this Sir. We'll just have to flush him out. And we can do that. One of my Traffic Wardens, Keith, will explain Prime Minister. Shall we go to Police HQ sir?"

Chapter Thirty

The air of panic in the County Police Control Room could be cut with a knife. Slippery Liz had bollocked everyone in sight and was still demanding to know from a very harassed Monty, exactly where the PM was now. At this minute! The Home Secretary was on his way to the Police HQ also demanding to know the PM's current whereabouts and threatening Liz with several dire consequences if she didn't tell him. She wasn't sure whether she was relieved or scared shitless when the very same PM came bounding through the door of the control room followed by his bodyguard and Barbara and headed straight towards her.

"Chief Constable. An office please. Now, if you don't mind. At this minute Chief Constable. Not tomorrow." She looked round wildly and ushered the new arrivals and Monty into the office reserved for her when she was at the HQ, and shut the door behind her. The noise of the busy control room receded and quiet reigned. For a short while.

"Well Chief constable. Tell me what's going on? As you can see, I'm still alive, but no thanks to you I might add."

Liz gulped and looked at him in horror. His surprise presence indicated to her fevered brain that she really hadn't a clue what was going on. She thought he was still in his hotel. She sat down heavily and wiped her brow.

"Prime Minister, may I explain on behalf of the Chief Constable?" Asked Monty quietly. He had overseen the arrests and incarceration of the prisoners from the Old Manse and had become increasingly worried about who the hell they all were. But at least he had some theories he could offer the Prime Minister. Liz obviously didn't have the foggiest.

"No you can't Chief Superintendent, because you don't know anything useful either. In fact, to cut matters short, the head Traffic Warden, Barbara here will explain exactly what has been going on over the past few weeks, because neither you, nor the SAS or the Police, or anyone else for that matter except the Traffic Wardens have a clue about any of it. Barbara. Please go ahead."

"Before I tell you that Sir, let me introduce you to a terrorist." She smiled again as Reggie shuffled into the room, looking nervous, hangdog and downright scared. "Reggie Parkes Prime Minister." Reggie had arrived at Police HQ about ten minutes before in the cone van and had reluctantly been persuaded to meet the PM.

The Prime Minister, ever the politician, knew instinctively when to get people on his side and instill loyalty, stood up. "Mr Parkes. The first thing I have to ask you is; have you heard from Roxy? I'm worried about her."

Reggie looked at him hard, expecting him to take the piss out of himself or Roxy. PM or no PM, he wouldn't stand for that.

"Your niece was helping the staff at the Old Manse, and indeed was helping me to write a speech for today's television interview. A remarkably bright young girl, your niece. Got good brains you know and she can write really stirring stuff." He looked sideways at Barbara as if for approval.

Reggie's face softened as he heard these fine words. Of course! That was it. It was her brains they were after. Speech writing. He'd always liked the speeches made by this PM even if they were political and therefore total rubbish. But they said the right things at the right time. Roxy's work no doubt. And all those other bastards insinuating… well, insinuating other things; rude things about her. Well he should have known. They were always wrong. She's as white as the driven snow. But then he thought, wait a moment, where is the girl? He looked round in panic. The PM was right. Where was Roxy? She could have been burnt in that house fire. He was about to make for the phone on the nearby desk to ring the police just as Roxy herself burst into the room.

"Uncle Reggie!" she exclaimed in a high-pitched voice and flung herself into his arms. "Oh Uncle, thank God you're safe." She smothered Reggie with kisses, and delighted as he always was with this adorable girl, he had to extricate himself from her embrace in order to breathe. Even if he went to prison after all this shit and aggro, Reggie was now a happy man.

Roxy released him eventually and looked round the room. Satisfied that Reggie was OK, she was ready to talk to the others. "Oh, hello Prime Minister. All good?"

"All very good Roxy thank you. But I'm going to have to change my speech a bit. Barbara here has been telling me all about your uncle. A very enterprising man indeed. Roxy, why don't you take Mr Parkes up to the café on the second floor for a cup of tea? We'll be finished here in a few minutes with this police business and then we can all get on with life as they say." He stood and saw Roxy and Reggie out, offering Roxy a furtive wink as they left the room before turning back to his seat.

"Now come along everybody else, let's sit down. We were just talking about who the real culprit in all this is. Barbara? Please continue."

Monty sighed. A few more hours and he'd have sorted it out himself. He knew it was the bloody Traffic Wardens.

Twenty minutes later, Barbara finished her tale. "...... so the reason we couldn't tell anyone was simply because at first even we didn't know. Reggie was scared stiff after the Percy Smythe incident and decided to hide up, and I don't blame him. And then, even when we did know, we couldn't tell anyone because the package would have been taken off us by Percy's lot and that would have been that. A rotten arms sale, blackmail to keep the Prime Minister quiet, and all the rest of it. It was all exaggerated out of nothing by that reporter, who got the wrong end of the stick about everything, and it has only ended now because the Traffic Wardens decided to take a hand." She had left out the full details of the PM and the teenies, merely explaining that there were scenes of him engaged in anti-government demonstrations as a young student which would be especially embarrassing to him now so soon before an election.

Barbara sat down and looked around at the collection of stunned senior policemen and women. The silence lasted for less than 5 seconds before everyone started speaking at the same time.

"I simply don't believe….."

"Can't be true. Think of all the cost….."

"Shitty death……" This last from Liz herself.

The hubbub ceased immediately as the Home Secretary burst into the room.

"Ah, thank God you're OK Gerry," he said to the Prime Minister. "I was so worried. There was rumour you'd been attacked by terrorists at the Old Manse." He looked round the room, surprised to see the assembled officials. Even a Traffic Warden sitting there!

"Cuthbert! How nice to see you. I wondered where you'd got to. Do sit down and help us sort out a problem."

"Of course old boy. Of course. But I'm still anxious to sort out these damned terrorists, and of course find a flash drive that's gone missing. It might contain the key to all this. Surely we need to concentrate on that. The Chief Constable here can brief you about the situation here on the ground."

"Do you mean this flash drive Cuthbert?" The Home Secretary jumped as the PM fished the drive from his pocket and held it up for all to see.

"Prime Minister, you have it. How……………." He began to stutter in his confusion. He couldn't for a moment think straight. One minute, the drive was firmly in the hands of terrorists and even his own highly trained men hadn't been able to retrieve it, and now here it was in the hands of the Prime Minister himself! Then his mind cleared. His men had obviously been successful in some way and had got it off Reggie and given it to the PM. Good. He must get it back to London.

"Yes Cuthbert, the Police captured all the terrorists at the Old Manse, including Reggie Parkes. And the silly fool had it on him."

"What terro……." He stopped. His own men had been there under Archie Fitzpaine. Had they been captured? A million thoughts crowded into his mind, but one thought predominated. All that could be sorted out later. Right now, he had to get that drive.

The Prime Minister broke the silence. "It's OK though, there doesn't appear to be anything on it and what there is, has a password protection. Too difficult for our local people here to crack."

"I had it protected Prime Minister." The Home Secretary was now on firmer ground and was relieved to hear that all was safe and that no-one had seen what was on the drive. "It's mainly MI5 administrative stuff, payroll matters and staff dispositions and so on, but nevertheless best not discussed here. There's nothing mind blowing on it, I can assure you. It was sent by post to me from our West Country outlier. There's a bit of surveillance information, and some of it is sensitive, which is why we wanted it back so urgently. Can't have that sort of thing going missing. Just think of the press! My staff have the codes. When they've sorted the information, I'll give you a full briefing. I suppose I'd better get it up to London with one of my men right away. The Chief Constable seems to have everything in hand down here, so we'd probably best carry on with the programme."

He held his hand out for the drive.

"Yes of course Cuthbert, take it and send it up to town. Tell me all about it later."

The Home Secretary seemed to breathe a huge sigh of relief as he took the drive. "I'll just go and hand it over to one of my staff outside. It'll now be perfectly safe, don't worry Prime Minister." He marched to the door and disappeared out of the room, his step purposeful and confident. As he moved, he inspected the drive to make sure the tiny ID mark on the drive base was there. He inspected it carefully. 'Yes" he thought. The mark is there, and the small mark on the slide out section. It's the right one OK, he thought with relief.

Keith had been particularly careful on that point.

The Prime Minister Looked round the room, still unwilling to believe the obvious. He sat down, sighing.

"Well Ladies and Gentlemen! That's that then! He lied, didn't he? Over to you Liz. I don't want him back in the room. Arrest him quietly. Take him to London and hand him over to the Met. House arrest. No fuss. No contact with anyone. No media of any kind. Not until I've seen him. There are precedents after all. The security of the realm is at stake here. He'll have to resign of course. Oh, and don't worry about the flash drive. That one was a fake." He held up the real one. "And I will be holding on to this one." He closed his eyes in weariness, then seemed to come alive again. He was OK. He could spin all this easily. It could win him the next election. Terrorists defeated. Done deal! He looked at the chief constable who was still staring at the flash drive. No one had moved. The Prime Minister, unused to any form of slackness spoke again, his voice ice cold.

Liz? Move it. The Home Secretary? Sort it, please. Now!"

Liz dragged her eyes off the drive that they had all been searching for what seemed like years, and nodded to Dibsey. Dibsey stood up and left the room quietly.

"Now, Liz, get that reporter woman in here. Once I've sorted her out, we can get on with the rest of the programme, although modified a bit perhaps." He stood up grinning, very much the genial PM again.

Chapter Thirty One

Reggie Parkes QGM and his new wife, Phyllis Elworthy-Parkes, stepped out on to the steps of the Parksdown Registry Office and into the warm autumn sunshine of a glorious English day. Two lines of Traffic Wardens, ticket books held aloft formed an arch under which the happy couple walked. They reached Phyllis's ribbon bedecked Lada and with a rattle of tin cans set off to the fully refurbished Pig and Whistle pub that had been contracted to cater for the reception. Deidre, fully recovered from the shock of the cone van incident had volunteered to mastermind the proceedings and ensure a good time was held by all. It was only right. She knew the Wardens; knew of their little and large peccadilloes, and after all, had even had one of their cone vans drive right up to her bar!

A lot had happened since the Prime Minister had held his meeting in the Police Headquarters. Soon after the meeting had finished, Jennifer Johnson received a shock when she answered her phone only to be summoned to Police HQ by no less than the Chief Superintendent himself. Used to being told to fuck off by the police and just about everyone else in the emergency services, she was a bit wary at first, and was even more suspicious when a large squad car appeared outside the newspaper office with lights flashing.

The constable was polite but firm. "You can come with us now miss if you want, or not. It's up to you. The Prime Minister wants you to interview him about the present terrorist situation in Westbourne. We are here to make sure you get there safely. Or we can get hold of another reporter of course. Your choice."

Disgorged from the police car and escorted into the Prime Minister's presence, Jennifer was frantic to think of some grown up and mature questions to ask. After all, this was the Prime Minister, the leader of the nation. What she said in her report would be spread nationwide. No, worldwide! Everybody would read it. Absolutely everybody. The whole world was already following this saga with great interest.

The Prime Minister stood as she entered the control room office. "Ah, Miss Johnson. I've heard a lot about you. You are evidently the one who knows most about this situation the town finds itself in. Please sit down and we can start."

An hour and a half later, she had written her report. Half an hour after that, the early edition of the paper went out on sale. She knew she had made it. Just before publication of her piece in the Gazette, a representative from Global News Corp in London had offered her a job as Chief Political Editor World desk. New York or London. Her choice. Minutes later, the editor of 'Goodbye Privacy' a global celebrity gossip magazine also rang with an offer of a Senior Editor position. She surprised even herself when she turned both down. Her own newspaper group proprietor, Sir Archibald Ponsonby-Greenwald, had offered her the post of Editor in Chief and Chief Executive of Southern Global Group, which included her own local town paper, the Westbourne Gazette, which in turn covered editorship of a large number of subsidiary newspapers throughout the West Country. Her own paper! Her very own organisation! The top boss! Larger outfits could come later. At Southern, she would be Number One.

Her final report on the incident, after the PM's interview was fair and succinct, and very successful, with syndication all over the world.

Terrorists Captured
Prime Minister Calms the Situation
**An exclusive interview with the Prime Minister by
Jennifer Johnson
Senior Editor**

The Prime Minister today called on everyone in the country to congratulate the forces of law and order, and the armed services for their success in ending a terrorist plot that at one time threatened the very safety of the realm. Police forces backed up by the army last night captured a number of terrorists in a daring night raid on the Old Manse, on the Welford Road just outside of Westbourne. Several of them were treated in hospital for minor injuries. None of the security forces were hurt. The Prime Minister hailed it as a major success in the fight against global terrorism and thanked the hero of the day, Traffic Warden Reggie Parkes, who undertook the dangerous role of undercover agent in the terrorist organisation. Constantly at risk of his life, Mr Parkes, whom we already know as a hero in a recent diamond robbery incident, has been recommended for the award of the Queen's Gallantry Medal for his part in the defeat of the terrorists.

The Police have established that none of the terrorists are British, and the Prime Minister has assured me that all of them will be immediately repatriated to their own countries to stand trial despite any possible interference by the European Court of Justice. In fact, it is believed that they have already departed the UK. He stated that "it is time we did what is best for this great country of ours without interference from others. These people were here illegally and now they've gone, we'll never hear of them again."

In a surprise announcement, the Home Secretary, Cuthbert Montgomery has resigned. He told the press that despite the success of the recent terrorist operation and his evident popularity in Parliament, he felt that it had brought home the fact that he had very little family time and he now wanted to concentrate on that for the next few years while his children grow up. The Prime Minister has most regretfully accepted his resignation after failing to persuade him to remain in post.

In another development, Dame Elizabeth Longstaff, Chief Constable of the County has also resigned her position. We believe her motive may be to stand for Parliament following the resignation of the Home Secretary. The Prime Minister praised her work in playing a leading role in defeating the terrorists and has made it quite plain that he would welcome her application to join the local party organisation.

The Prime Minister had been thorough with his people. He had left nothing to chance. It wasn't the first time he had had to put a bit of spin around a situation and then had to put a bit of gloss on that spin. And then cover the whole lot in sugar. He knew it was the only way to stay in power and keep at bay those sodding backbenchers and the truly evil opposition. His interview with the Home Secretary had been totally one sided.

"Resign or I'll explain all. And don't think for a second Cuthbert that you can wriggle out of this one. You have nothing on me. I have everything on you. My bit with the teenies on the flash drive is no more. Your dirty fingerprints on the other hand are all over it. And I'll be keeping it as evidence, in a safe place where even your brutes can't reach it. Everyone heard the lie you told in the Police Ops room, and you'll resign, or go to prison. I'd prefer it if you didn't go to prison for political reasons obviously, as you might be tempted to spill a few beans, and it won't look good for the party, but I'm sure you won't want prison either. It's not nice in those places, especially if one of my associates spreads the word about certain of your habits. So this is the deal. You resign as Home Secretary and retire from politics for health or family reasons, and I'll forget all about your treacherous part in this."

The Home Secretary resigned and retired and the Prime Minister moved on the Chief Constable.

He welcomed Liz to the Office with a broad grin on his face. His interview with her was rather one sided as well. "Well Chief Constable? Come in. Sit down. A bad situation turned good for all of us if we are able to grasp opportunities when they pop up eh? You have options here, unlike the Home Secretary even though your part in this drama wasn't very impressive, I have to say. You didn't have a clue about what was going on really, and to be quite frank Liz my girl, in short, you didn't shine. But I do know your pedigree and your politics and should you resign and stand for Parliament, I'll back you. If not? Well, I've enough on you to at least shift you sideways to an admin post in London, maybe even with a small demotion. I mean, it's not entirely up to me, but I think I have some say in the matter, and I think the person I appoint to be the new Home Secretary will listen to me. So will you grasp this opportunity Liz old girl? C'mon! You're a sneaky, devious bitch. You remind me of a female version of me, and the country needs people like us in politics, and anyway, I think you could go far. It's a once in a lifetime opportunity by the way, so what I'm saying is that I want you to resign as Chief Constable of the County. Now! Right now! Here in this room. Here's the paper. Just sign here."

Liz opened her mouth to speak. "Yes or no Liz" interrupted the Prime Minister before she could speak. "This is a time sensitive, one time offer. You've got ten seconds to decide. I've got to get back to London and I've got a country to run. So what's your answer? Do you want to sign? Ten, nine…." He looked meaningfully at his watch.

Liz signed.

"Oh, and before you actually depart Liz; that Brightwell character. He's still quite young, and he seems to have a lot of 'go' in him, but he needs a dose of reality and lot of sharpening up. Have him transferred to the Met for a couple of years on secondment will you. It'll make or break him. Then if he comes back in one piece, he might be of some use to someone."

The Prime Minister finished his day in Westbourne by calling in on Monty, and then on Barbara. He was gentle with Monty. At least the man was on his way to solving the puzzle of the terrorists and Traffic Wardens. At least he had some clue about what was going on and at least he was a thinker. And he had been a damned good copper throughout his long career. "Well Chief Superintendent," he said as Monty entered the room, "I understand you are thinking of retiring? Probably as well because I can't offer you the County I'm afraid; not after this debacle."

"I expected as much sir. I had hoped it would end under better circumstances than this balls up, but there we are. I got it wrong. Can't have it all ways I suppose. But I've had a damned good time in the force and won't ever regret my career choice, so no regrets really." He looked glumly out of the window. He really did wish it hadn't come to this though. He'd done well in his career and it was such a shame to end on this bad note. And poor Doris! Well, he'd try and keep the worst from her, and he would make sure that they really enjoyed their retirement together. Some travel perhaps. More time with the grandchildren.

"Come now Chief Superintendent. Not all bad is it? Can't have you getting bitter and twisted in your old age. I'm sure none of us want any of this raked up in the future. I mean, the costs involved! That RAF AWACs aircraft alone cost two million pounds for its short time over Westbourne! The Chancellor had a fit because it all had to come out of the contingency fund! So, I hope we can rely on your absolute discretion in future. And if it helps Monty, I think the matter of a certain very high honour in the New Year's list might be acceptable to you and Doris eh? For excellent services to this country over a long period. After all, as you said, you've had a damned good career as a policeman, and you were right about that."

Monty looked round, visibly brightening. Of course, he thought. The PM is going to want all this kept absolutely quiet. He won't want his legacy ruined by the exposure of a complete and very expensive farce. On the other hand, he didn't want his own legacy as a fine police officer ruined either by having to retire in ignominy. A knighthood would definitely solve both problems. In effect, they both had each other by the short and curlies. He would retire with a visible honour and he'd keep his mouth firmly shut. The PM wouldn't be embarrassed in the future by any leaks about what really had happened. Not from him anyway. He looked with renewed admiration at this man who knew how to gain loyalty from good people - and keep it.

"You're right sir," he replied with a wide grin. "It certainly would help. And thank you. La…" He stopped short, just avoiding saying in advance 'Lady Doris.' He could wait for that pleasure until the New Year. "Er, both Doris and I would be very happy indeed with that sir."

The Prime Minister knew he would be.

As for Barbara, the PM was equally generous. After all, out of all of them, she was the one who had sorted it all out. Sorted out the worst shambles he'd ever got himself involved in. Without her and her Traffic Wardens, he could now be the laughing stock of the entire world and sitting on the back benches, with probably that treacherous shit of a Home Secretary as Prime Minister.

"Well Barbara. I can only offer my thanks for a job well done. And bravely done. And this isn't political bullshit or spin. I did all that with the others. I really admire your guts and intelligence. You did more than well, and your team backed you up to the hilt. I only wish we had such loyalty in politicians." He broke off laughing. "That van in the pub business, and the naked terrorist. I mean it's the stuff of comedy, isn't it. It's bloody funny looking back. But seriously, do you realise what could have happened had you not taken over. OK, I would have been sunk, that's true, but so would the dignity of the nation, and believe me, most decent politicians - and there are some, would tell you that that is of far more importance than just me being badly embarrassed."

Barbara was a bit sceptical about that, but it did seem that the PM was doing his very best to sort out everyone involved in what became known as the 'Westbourne Terror'.

"Anyway, I understand you'll be retiring soon. I'll be sorry to see you go. Genuinely, but at least it is within my powers to grant you an enhanced pension. Considerably enhanced, as well as recommending an honour from Her Majesty in the New Year's list. A high honour I might add, that will ensure your recognition for services bloody well done, but not to be talked about. By the way, on that same subject, as you may have seen in the papers, I've made an immediate recommendation that the QGM be awarded to Mr Parkes. He thoroughly deserves it in a strange sort of way. I mean, he's no hero as we all know, but there again, he was there in the thick of it all, facing real danger and aggro without giving up. And that's really the best type of hero I guess. One who keeps going and doing his duty, even though he's scared witless. He was frightened, alone and worried about his mum and his chinchillas, whatever they are. A type of rat I suppose. And he stuck it out with the help of his new wife. Strange how things turn out isn't it. Talking of his chinchillas. Did they survive all this?"

"They did sir. His mum had asked a friend to look after them before the fire took the house, as Reggie had moved in with his Phyllis and was unable to keep an eye on them. And yes, he does deserve well of us. But he is of course homeless now sir. They are staying at my sister's flat at the moment."

"Oh, don't worry about the housing situation Barbara. The compensation money for Parkes and his new wife will more than cover them for a new house, plus extras, plus five star hotel accommodation until they get sorted out if your sister needs her flat in the meantime. Roxy told me all about their fears on that score, and the Government always pays its dues to the deserving. Sometimes."

"That's good Sir. I was a bit worried about that."

She had also been worried what it would be like in the crew room with Reggie with a wound and a medal, and a certain notoriety as a hero, but pushed the thought to the back of her minds as being unworthy. He did indeed deserve a hero's welcome anytime in that crew room and she was prepared to wait and see what happened. After all, she was retiring soon anyway.

But when it came, surprisingly, Reggie seemed to have changed. In the first daily briefing since the incident, he had sat at the back of the morning crew briefing in silence. Just sat there, taking it all in, but offering none of the usual Reggie type opinionated crap of old. He told

Barbara later that it wasn't just the influence of Phyllis, albeit she was the most wonderful person to come into his life since Roxy. He told her that when he had nothing to boast about, he needed to boast. He needed some sort of recognition even if it was his own, so that he wouldn't believe himself a failure and a nonentity, consigned to living with his old mum and two chinchillas forever. Now he had recognition, and a wound, and a medal, and a wife, and even though he knew himself that he was no hero at all, he didn't need to boast anymore. He knew that he had at the very least, done OK, and he knew that other people knew. And that was enough for him.

She had made some changes in the ranks of her wardens in the past week. Dan had been brought in from the cold. She had explained his role as snitch of falsehoods to Dibsey and others to the rest of the crew. Two cone vans were now to be operated and Dan would be overall van team leader with Jan as his deputy and second van driver. Both were happy. Dave and Jan were now an item which is why Barbara kept Dave with Dan and assigned Polly to Jan's van.

Polly and Henrietta renewed their fight about the bit of banana on the floor of the ladies, and Keith was rewarded with a Police Commendation for Excellence and received an offer to become a lecturer in computer science at Westbourne University; an offer he gladly accepted. The cone violence episode was still deeply embedded in his mind and a life in academia seemed a much safer option than life on the streets. Boobs persuaded himself that he had played a major part in the unfolding events because after all, it was obvious that the ploy with the SAS team had worked only because of his acting ability, and he applied to be the front half of the camel in the forthcoming Christmas play. He had some revenge to exact.

All in all, the Traffic Warden crew was happy and settled again for the first time in months and Barbara felt it was the right time to announce her retirement on such a high note. She was sixty five and times were changing in the Traffic Warden world. The Police had relinquished control of the wardens a few years back and the Council had taken over. They were officially Civil Enforcement Officers now and hand held, electronic machines had taken over from ticket books. It all seemed to work and she accepted that, but something had been lost she thought. Same great people; same dedication; but just something missing in the setup. The Police badge perhaps? The loss of ticket books. Or was she just old fashioned. She didn't exactly know, but she did now feel it was the right time to go with no regrets, and let new people take over. Like Monty, she had also had a damned good career and was ready for a rest. She had told the Wardens that she didn't know who would be her successor, and in her heart, she really didn't know or care.

The Council would decide in due course, which gave no one any confidence at all, and she shed an unaccustomed tear when Dan told over a whisky at her going away do that not a single Traffic Warden wanted her to go.

Several days after the wedding, and the very successful reception at the Pig and Whistle, Reggie, Phyllis and Roxy sat at the pavement café outside the Royal Hotel in Westbourne, each with a glass in their hands. Muggins, tied fast to a chair leg so that he wouldn't savage passers-by, glowered at their feet. They were waiting for Reggie's mum to appear. She was in the hotel at a meeting organised by the South of England Computer Hackers' Society, of which she was now an honorary member. She never said much at meetings, for obvious reasons, but had been asked by a splinter group of the Society to give a demonstration of how to hack into Pentagon files which she was now doing.

The small group outside we're happy to wait in the sun of a lovely autumn day, enjoying their drinks.

"Well, Uncle Reggie, I'm off to London again next week," said Roxy. "The PM wants to see me again."

"What for this time Roxy; another speech?" Reggie looked at her proudly. His own niece writing speeches for the Prime Minister himself. He was so proud of her. His eyes moistened as he leaned forward to speak to her.

"You just make sure that PM treats you right Roxy," he said gruffly. "Make sure he sees to all your needs."

"He definitely does that Uncle."

"You see Phyllis," said Reggie relaxing back into his chair and taking a gulp of his beer. "That Prime Minister wants her brains again."

"Yeah, something like that Uncle" said Roxy and grinned at Phyllis.

Phyllis grinned back and raised her glass. "Come on, let's drink a toast to that."

They raised their glasses together; a happy, ordinary, family group, sitting in the sunshine of a fine English day, in the peaceful, terrorist free town of Westbourne.

"To the Prime Minister and Roxy's brains," they chorused as one.

www.ingramcontent.com/pod-product-compliance
Lightning Source LLC
Chambersburg PA
CBHW051555030726
47592CB00001B/294